W9-AAD-239

EXIT INTO ETERNITY

Tales of the Bizarre and Supernatural

by

C.M. EDDY, JR.

With an Introduction by

MURIEL E. EDDY

FENHAM PUBLISHING
NARRAGANSETT, R. I.

Published by
Fenham Publishing, LLC
P.O. Box 767
Narragansett, RI 02882

First Fenham Publishing trade edition October 2000

10 9 8 7 6 5 4 3 2 1

Originally published in hardcover by the Eddy family 1973

Library of Congress Control Number: 00-136061

ISBN 0-9701699-0-6

Cover Design: Lesa Nash

Printing and Binding: Warwick Press, Warwick, RI

Cover Photo: James W. Dyer

Author Photo: Courtesy of the Eddy family collection

Printed in the United States of America

INTRODUCTION

I met Clifford Martin Eddy, Jr. through our mutual interest in creative writing. We were both avid readers, and our letters to editors appeared in several of the same magazines. Soon we began corresponding with each other.

Following our marriage in 1918, we continued with our writing activities. Cliff's chief interests were detective tales, stories about songwriting, and ghost stories. I wrote romantic adventure and occult experience pieces.

Some of Cliff's work which was published during the early part of our marriage included: SIGN OF THE DRAGON, story of a female detective, *Mystery Magazine*, 1919; A LITTLE BIT OF GOOD LUCK, story about songwriting, *Munsey's Magazine*, 1920; MOONSHINE, a ghost story, *Action Stories*, 1922; THE UNSHORN LAMB, about songwriting, *Snappy Stories*, 1922.

Cliff and I met Howard Philips Lovecraft in 1923. We were introduced by their mothers, who were both active in the women's suffrage movement.

During their early friendship, Cliff was influenced greatly by Howard's interest in the weird and supernatural. While I was busy taking care of our three children, Cliff took many trips with Howard, either by trolley or on foot, to interesting places in Rhode Island---the Old Stone Mill in Newport, to find a hidden swamp in Chepachet, and through the historic streets of Providence.

I typed many of Howard's manuscripts, and he read them to us in his sepulchral voice, usually well past the midnight hour.

Howard's professorial style of writing became evident in the stories Cliff wrote over the next few years. Howard was very generous in his suggestions for more vivid, imaginative passages, and in some instances did the actual revisions.

Three of these revised stories appeared in *Weird Tales* during 1924 and 1925. THE GHOST EATER, a gray wolf at full moon, 1924; THE LOVED DEAD, demoniac desire for the dead, 1924; DEAF, DUMB, AND BLIND, chronicle of Satanic sensations, 1925.

Other stories by Cliff which appeared in *Weird Tales* during 1924 and 1925 were: ASHES, experiment by a chemistry professor, 1924; WITH WEAPONS OF STONE, a story of prehistoric man, 1924; ARHL-A OF THE CAVES, prehistoric man, 1925; THE BETTER CHOICE, machine for reviving dead, 1925.

With the demise of *Weird Tales*, placing stories of the macabre and fantastic became difficult, and many manuscripts by my husband were put away while he sought other work to support the family. He had always been interested in the theater, and soon became active in the entertainment field, producing talent shows in theaters throughout Rhode Island, Massachusetts and Connecticut.

He also collaborated with others in writing music, both lyrics and melodies. Some of his more widely circulated published songs were "Dearest of All," "When We Met by the Blue Lagoon," "In My Wonderful Temple of Love," "Wonderful Sunset Hour."

Cliff was employed in the proofreading department of Oxford Press for several years, and in the business management office of the Rhode Island Department of Public Works for almost ten years.

He served as treasurer and later president of the R.I. Writers' Guild. A manuscript he wrote while Guild President entitled FACTS AND FICTION ABOUT CREATIVE WRITING was printed in booklet form.

I wrote an article about our friendship with Howard Lovecraft as one of the pieces for a booklet, *Rhode Island on Lovecraft*, and later published a full profile of HPL, THE GENTLEMAN FROM ANGELL STREET. I have written other articles about Howard, including THE HOWARD PHILLIPS LOVECRAFT WE KNEW, and THE MAN AND THE IMAGE.

Howard had corresponded with August Derleth, a Wisconsin writer, for many years. After HPL's death in 1937, my husband and I started to correspond with August. He became a dear friend to us both, and called at our home during two brief visits to Providence.

August first reprinted THE LOVED DEAD by Arkham House Publishers, in 1948, and it has been reprinted many times. In 1966, he reprinted three stories of Cliff's--- THE LOVED DEAD, THE GHOST EATER, and DEAF, DUMB, AND BLIND in *The Dark Brotherhood*. Cliff wrote an article especially for this book entitled WALKS WITH H.P. LOVECRAFT.

Howard and Cliff had both done ghost-writing for the master magician, Houdini. They had researched and prepared a manuscript for him entitled THE CANCER OF SUPER-STITION which was never published due to Houdini's death in 1926. This appeared for the first time in *The Dark*

Brotherhood.

Howard had introduced Cliff to Houdini, and I introduced Howard to a writer named Hazel Heald in Massachusetts. These contacts proved successful for all. In addition to Cliff's ghost-writing for Houdini, he also worked closely with him in the exposure of fake spiritualistic mediums.

Howard helped Mrs. Heald with her stories, and she placed several in *Weird Tales*. Hazel died in 1961, but reprints of her fiction are included in "The Horror in the Museum," published in hard cover by Arkham House.

As the years passed, Cliff and I focused our efforts on literary criticism, although we continued with creative writing as an avocation.

In 1967 Cliff started BLACK NOON, an imaginative fictionalized parallelism of his adventures with Howard, but he was unable to complete it due to illness. He passed away later that year. August Derleth was intending to finish this work, and perhaps expand it into a full length novel but it remained unfinished due to August's death in 1971.

Cliff was always interested in the idea of parallel planes—where life on another level, either astral or otherwise, would be similar to that on earth---or where life might exist, but in another time or another form. He was also fascinated by the themes of teleportation, vampirism, ghosts and the mystery of unexplained phenomena. He was an avid student of mythology and mysticism, and he spent hours in the library researching the unusual, the unique, the bizarre.

The stories included in this volume, reflect Cliff's

ability to weave unusual plots based on his thorough research and lively imagination.

PILGRIMAGE OF PERIL and THE VENGEFUL VISION were written in 1924, during the Lovecraftian association. MISCREANT FROM MURANIA, based on intensive research, was completed by Cliff in 1951. A SOLITARY SOLUTION was also written in 1924, possibly Cliff's most productive period of creativity. BLACK NOON, started by Cliff in 1967, appears in its unfinished form.

Students in many high schools and colleges are now studying literature of the macabre and supernatural. I hope that this volume will serve as an interesting source of reference for them, and also provide exciting reading for others.

Muriel E. Eddy

CONTENTS

Pilgrimage of Peril

FOREWORD

HAD I NOT BEEN a personal friend of Professor Everett Z. Greyland for years, and thoroughly cognizant of the marvelous progress made by the organization of which he was the president; had I not absolute faith in Professor Greyland's integrity and truthfulness, I would never have written the accompanying story.

The account of the epoch-making meeting of the Spiritist Club of America, at which Mr. Joseph Carson proposed the startling undertaking and performed the experiment which surprised the foremost psychologists in America---has been taken carefully from the records of the Society for February 11, 1930.

The data regarding the experiment in Professor Greyland's home, from the gathering of the seven on February eighteenth to the return of the astral wanderer on February twenty-second, have been supplied by the Professor himself and have been substantiated by his five colleagues.

The astounding tale of Joe Carson was reconstructed by me from the notes made by Professor Greyland, which were read by him at the meeting of the Inner Circle on February twenty-fifth and certified by the quintette who assisted him in the experiment. By unanimous vote, this account was incorporated into the records of the Club, being duly received by Dr. Arthur M. Lackall, the Club's secretary.

On March tenth, a special meeting of the Inner Circle was called, and it was voted unanimously to publish this narrative, with the following notice:

"It is the thought of the Club that perhaps this tale will reach someone who has all the necessary attributes to engage in a similar experiment---youth, a mind schooled in the higher sciences, a strong physique, and a freedom from family ties---someone who will join forces with these earnest workers in an effort to learn the fate of that intrepid explorer, Joe Carson.

"If such a person reads this story he may secure more detailed information from Dr. Lackall or Professor Greyland."

The following account appeared in a subsequent issue of the Spiritist Club's national publication, but unfortunately it did not bring forth the desired results.

The reader, therefore, must draw his own conclusions, scientific or otherwise, until such a time as history can record the facts through other astral journeyings.

Sincerely,
C. M. Eddy, Jr.

CHAPTER I
THE SPIRITIST CLUB

The newcomer had been under the scrutiny of two score pair of eyes ever since Professor Greyland had shown him into the club room earlier in the evening. It was an unwritten law among them that no visitor should be allowed at any of the regular meetings of the organization unless he was a prospective member, and the Professor's companion seemed rather young to qualify for a place among them. Still, this was a place where knowledge, rather than age, counted, so the members held their counsel 'till their leader should volunteer an explanation.

The young man seemed totally unconscious of the sensation he was creating. He followed with eager interest the reports of the scientists as each was read in turn. His eyes gleamed with understanding whenever a zealous member warmed to the subject at hand and launched into a highly technical dissertation on the particular branch of occult phenomena it had been his province to investigate.

At length the last report had been read and approved. A hush fell upon the gathering as the old Professor took his place upon the platform.

"Gentlemen, it has been the good fortune of most of you to have been with this organization since its inception some ten years ago. All of us, I know, have been subjected to the incredulous sneers of the skeptical majority but, armed with a courage born of conviction, secure in the strength of our wisdom, we have forged resolutely ahead, our goal always the better understanding of the so-called mysteries of life and the fuller development of the science known among ourselves as astral projection.

"During this decade, tremendous strides have been made. For the benefit of our newer members I beg your indulgence while I briefly outline a few of the things we have been doing---things which were pronounced impossible a few short years ago and which, even now, are looked upon by many as being too fanatical, too improbable to be granted serious consideration.

"In the first place, we have conclusively proven that it is possible for the soul of man to leave his physical body. I vouchsafe that each one of you here, tonight, has tested this to his own satisfaction; that each one of you has essayed a pilgrimage into the astral spheres."

Two score heads nodded in silent assent. The Professor cleared his throat, and continued:

We felt that we had reached the pinnacle of our achievement about a year ago, when Brother Elsner launched still further into the unknown and proved that it was physically possible for the soul of man to occupy two separate bodies; the one remaining in a trance-like state, while the other was being inhabited.

"But, now," he paused, impressively, "it has remained for an outsider, the young man I have brought with me this evening, to propound a theory far in advance of anything we have yet dreamed of accomplishing. Yet, recondite as his ideas may seem, they are hardly more esoteric than some of our own seemed before we succeeded in establishing the truth of them.

"I felt that it would be ethically unfair for me to

deprive this young man of the privilege of telling you in his own way about the experiment he is desirous of making. Therefore, I invited him to come along with me, that he might speak for himself.

"Gentlemen, it is with a sense of extreme gratification that I present to you a man after our own hearts---Mr. Joseph Carson."

The youth rose and made his way to the platform where he took a place at Professor Greyland's side. For the first time that evening he showed slight evidence of nervous excitement. He ran his fingers through his shock of black hair and a flush of embarrassment burned momentarily upon his cheeks.

The spectators appraised the newcomer and found him in no wise lacking. Six feet of clean-cut young manhood, with a warmth of personal magnetism that already was making itself felt upon those who studied him.

At a nod from the Professor, Joe Carson stepped into the place his host had vacated. The brief pause had been sufficient to allow him to regain his lost poise, and as he looked into the upturned faces of those learned men, he met their gaze unflinchingly. He spoke slowly, with a scarcely perceptible drawl.

"As my friend, the Professor, has indicated, since the days of the French followers of Mesmer, straight down through all the ensuing periods of clairvoyance, spiritism, occultism and their like; fraud and imposture have been so intermingled with scientifically proven facts that the lay mind has been unable to distinguish clearly between them. As a consequence, they have been discredited. As Sir Oliver Lodge has declared, and we all agree, I am sure, those who express disbelief in these things do not pronounce an opinion; they merely show ignorance.

"The keen analytical minds of the world are rapidly awakening to a realization of the full import and true seriousness of research along the high plane your efficient organization is pursuing. Their scoffings are giving way to awed silence in the face of the attested, incontrovertible discoveries you are making. A stride or two more along the path of progress and they will be won over to your side.

"As for me, gentlemen, I fear you will find that Professor Greyland has allowed his enthusiasm to run away with him. After listening to the recitals of your recent probings into the secrets of the higher sciences, I imagine that my theory will prove but a mere drop in the huge well of psychical research.

"If I understand aright, the keynote of all progress in the science of astral projection is the fact that all matter is subservient to the power of the mind. It is by mental concentration that the body is caused to remain dormant while the soul, by the same power, is released to go a-voyaging for hours, even days, at a time.

"It is merely a super-development of this mental power which has enabled one of your colleagues to make the progress your leader has cited.

"This being true, unless our premises are faulty in their very foundation, if the human body can be made to respond to the command of an all-powerful will, then my theory is only a logical one along the lines we are all following.

"Given the proper conditions, why could not the soul---which is the mind of man---summon the physical body to join it in some far distant place?

"This is the experiment I desire to attempt, the theory I hope to prove. I believe that it *is* possible, that the power of will is strong enough to overcome any material resistance; that the physical shell may be disintegrated, transmuted, by ethereal vibration, and restored intact, almost instantaneously, in some other part of the earth, even in some other sphere, at the call of the soul!

"Think what it would mean to the future of mankind if my theory can become a proven fact. Even the recent conquests of the air would pale into insignificance beside this great discovery. All of our present modes of travel would become obsolete. The inadequate devices of our men of vision for communicating with the other planets would no longer be necessary. Think of the great vista of possibilities that would be opened up along all other scientific lines."

The speaker paused amid a silence so intense that he could hear the stertorous breathing of his auditors. Professor Greyland's eyes were flashing pin-points of enthusiastic delight at the effect of his protégé's theoretical bombshell. He stroked his long beard with a satisfied smile.

Joe Carson watched the faces of the assemblage as the force of his words sank into their minds. He saw a few heads nod sagely at one another as he resumed the thread of his discourse:

"Of course, gentlemen, all of these things are a long way off. It will only be by years of earnest application that this perfection may ever be obtained. As yet, it is only an unsubstantiated theory.

"Do not think for a moment that I have underestimated the magnitude of the step I am about to take. It is because I fully appreciate the possibilities of failure that I come to you, tonight, seeking the cooperation of your more mature minds. Alone, I fear that I would be destined to fail. Together, I am equally sure that success must eventually come to us.

"But, after all, abstract theories amount to little. Material proof, even of supernatural truths, is necessary to gain recognition with the scientific mind. Before I can conscientiously ask you to ally yourselves with me in this undertaking, I feel I must offer you some concrete evidence that will convince you there is some vestige of truth in my assumptions.

"Professor Greyland has been kind enough to suggest that the little experiment I tried when I outlined my theory to him a few evenings ago, might be sufficient to dispel any doubts you might have as to the ultimate possibility of my plan."

Carson picked up a small table, and carried it down from the platform. The old Professor followed at his heels, bringing a chair.

"Now gentlemen," the youth directed, "I would like you all to form a circle about me. This will enable some of you to view me from every angle, and preclude the possibility of my practicing any form of deception."

There was a scraping of chairs as the scientists complied with his suggestion. The room was brilliantly illuminated, the light being distributed in such a manner that it fell upon the center of the circle from all sides, leaving a shadowless area.

Joe Carson removed his coat and rolled the sleeve of his shirt nearly all the way to his shoulder. He drew his chair up to the table, seated himself comfortably, and rested the full length of his bare, right arm upon the table top.

"You are all familiar with the process of self-hypnosis, by which the body is rendered inert, immobile, while the soul is released from the physical being. As that is necessarily the first step in the experiment I will start without further preamble. By the simple expedient of borrowing the voice of my physical self I hope to aid you in following the ensuing ones."

"Here was another startling innovation! To utilize the material voice as a means of communication between the astral and the physical world! Yet was it so radical a departure, after all? Spiritists and spiritualists had long maintained that it was the voice of the disembodied spirits that spoke through the mouths of the mediums. This youth was simply years ahead of the others in his theorems, that was all.

He rested his head against the back of the chair. The light gradually faded from his eyes leaving them blank, fixed, expressionless. At last the lids fluttered and drooped slowly over them. His head sagged over to one side. His breathing grew fainter and fainter until only the slight undulation of his breast bore witness that he was alive.

The super-sensitive minds of the scientists could actually feel the astral presence of Joe Carson as his ethereal body hovered above them .

"Now, gentlemen!" The voice seemed to come a great distance, yet each word was distinct and clear. At first they thought it the clever trick of a charlatan but, as the voice went steadily on, they lent eager ears.

"I am present located directly above Professor Greyland. I am going to request you to divide your attentions. The half of you who are on the same side of the circle as I, watch my hand and arm on the table. The others will please watch the area just over the Professor's head. If any of you care to note the time of your respective observations it might prove of value in testing my theory that the change is made instantaneously."

It was a full moment before anything happened. Then, trained to the mystical though they were, the onlookers could scarce repress a gasp of astonishment. A moment before there had been five fingers and a hand in full view upon the table. Now, only the stump of a wrist remained!

Even as they watched, the wrist and forearm as far as the elbow, disappeared---vanished into thin air!

But stranger even than this was the fact that simultaneously they reappeared in the air above Professor Greyland's head; first a finger, than a hand, 'till finally the whole arm to the elbow was materialized!

Slowly the hand and arm came lower 'till it was on a level with the circle of occultists. Then, in a weird, unaccountable manner, it moved from one to another while each examined it, made sure that it was not a mere illusion.

The circle completed, it disintegrated. Joe Carson, wide awake, his physical body whole once more, sat smiling at them from his vantage point at the table.

CHAPTER II
THE EXPERIMENT

A clock in a nearby tower boomed out the magic hour of midnight. The deep tones reverberated in the somber silence of the room, giving the final touch of mysticism to the scene.

Professor Greyland was on his feet the instant the echo of the last stroke died away. His voice shook with suppressed excitement as he once more addressed himself to his fellow members:

"The matter now rests in your hands, gentlemen. Shall we embrace this golden opportunity to delve deeper into the science we have made our life work, or shall we permit ourselves to hesitate, as I feel some of you are even now hesitating, because of your unwillingness to believe that one so young has the supreme mentality necessary to the culmination of so magnanimous a project? Should he fail, it will in no wise reflect upon us; while if he should succeed---". He paused as a grey-haired member rose and sought recognition.

"After witnessing Brother Carson's demonstration," the latter began, after formally addressing the chair, "I cannot believe that any one of us harbors any doubts as to his powers. I would suggest, however, that before we make any definite decision we ask our young friend if he has formulated any definite plan. "

A buzz of approval greeted his words. At a nod from the Professor, Joe Carson again took the floor. He was still smiling that same, enigmatical smile.

"You can readily understand how impossible it is to lay any hard and fast rules for such a venture. I think, though, that I can make clear the preliminary steps I consider essential.

"I propose that a few of you gentlemen, say half a dozen, be appointed to assist me. I shall expect the ones who are chosen to ally their powers of concentration with mine that, by our combined mental strength, by the added force such cooperation will give me, this physical body of mine shall be enabled to join me, out there." He waved his hand in an all-encompassing gesture.

"I do not feel that the first step of the experiment can possibly fail. The danger, as I see it, lies in my attempt to negotiate the return journey while so many miles from the source of my assistance." His smile this time was wry, whimsical. "I quite realize that failure will be synonymous with annihilation. That is the foremost reason why I think it better I should make the attempt, rather than one of you. I have youth, physical fitness, and I am entirely alone in the world.

"As for my ultimate destination, that I believe is one of the things that must be left to the exigencies of the situation. After all, It makes but little difference where I go, so long as I succeed in establishing the proof of my convictions. I propose to be guided in this by that higher Force of which we are all cognizant."

A brief discussion followed. When the meeting was adjourned, the occultists had unanimously placed their stamp of approval upon the proposed undertaking.

A week later, six staid spectacled scientists joined

Professor Greyland and Joe Carson in the formers study. A couch-bed occupied a salient position in the room, while on a tabouret stood a glass of water and a small circular box. Carson uncovered this and emptied four tiny dark-brown pellets into his outstretched palm.

"These tablets, gentlemen, contain in concentrated form nutritive elements sufficient to keep strength in the human body, while in the hypnotic state, for approximately four days. If I fail, I shall return to my physical shell within that time. If I succeed, I shall plan to return within the same four day limit if it is humanly possible for me to do so.

"Of course," he concluded, "it is thoroughly understood that at no time during the four days is this room to be left without the presence of one or more of you---even after my body has disappeared. Remember, my friends, my future safety may depend entirely upon your power of concentration and upon my being able to get into astral communication with you at an instant's notice."

One by one he placed the pellets upon his tongue, and washed each down with a sip from the glass.

"And, now, gentlemen, I think the time has come for me to bid you *adieu*."

He crossed to the cot, the scientists forming a circle about it. Fully dressed, he stretched his tall body at rest, and smiled up into the serious faces of the grey-bearded men who watched him; watched as his eyes closed, listened as his regular breathing died away to nothingness, watched until they seemed to see the subtle change that came over him as his soul departed, leaving the empty shell of his body behind.

Six minds joined to speed him on his pilgrimage of

peril; minds keenly attuned to the thought waves which would tell them when the first phase of the great experiment was at hand. Five hours later it came. Six pairs of earnest eyes watched the inert shell of Joe Carson with burning intensity, while the scientists bent every energy to the task at hand. One, long, poignant moment and it was over. Where the body of Joe Carson had stretched in deathlike repose was only a jumbled heap of empty clothes!

Professor Greyland gathered the garments reverently, tenderly and draped them across the back of a chair. In low tones they discussed the experiment advancing vague conjectures as to where the youth had gone and how long it would be before they would see him again---if ever! They argued as to the best method of assuring his safe return. At last it was decided to divide their vigil into three equal shifts of eight hours. This way, two of them would be in the room constantly, day and night; and the others would be within call at the first hint of the youth's attempted return.

Minutes stretched into hours, hours into days. Still no word or sign from the astral rover. Grave faces grew graver as the fourth day arrived. There would be no rest, now, for any of the sextette 'till the dawn of another day spelled either success or annihilation!

CHAPTER III
AN ETHEREAL WANDERER

Joe Carson's astral self lingered for a moment before drifting out into the great beyond and hovered over the heads of those upon whom so much depended. As their intellectual powers united to speed him on his way, flashes of blue, green and orange flooded the room with eerie shafts of lights; aura colors that stood for their supreme intellect, their steadfast truth and their untrammeled originality of thought. Already he could feel the electrifying effects of this amalgamation of power; already a new strength was surging through him, urging him on to his goal.

Reassured by this sense of loyalty, he willed his unshackled soul out into the night. Higher and higher he rose 'till the twinkling lights of the city below were like the tiny stars that shone in the heavens.

It was by no means the first time he had been upon some such nocturnal trip between heaven and earth, but somehow he found a greater joy than ever before in the freedom from bodily bondage. Perhaps it was because this trip was to be marked by unusual incident, perhaps he was thrilled by some occult premonition of the adventures which lay at the other end of his voyage. A sublime sense of peacefulness possessed him. He felt that he could drift idly on the gentle breeze forever.

For several moments he gave way to this feeling of lethargy, floating aimlessly upon the ever-changing currents of air, surcharged with a newborn mood of ecstatic joy.

But this soon passed. Once more that impelling force which found its inception in the super-sensitive minds upon the world below renewed his initiative, once again he felt himself spurred on to his mighty task .

He paused in mid-air in contemplation of what direction his journey was to lead him. Should he launch out upon a wild exploration of the tens of thousands of worlds that sparkled in the skies above him? Should he wing his way through countless miles of space beyond the moon, beyond the planets, beyond the visible stars and the milky way, beyond the unseen farther stars, and beyond the utmost limits of the material universe to those abysms of infinity no thought can reach and no imagination depict?

As if prompted by the thought itself he shot upward with the speed of a hurricane, but even as he sought to cross the limit of the earth's gravitation into the universe beyond, some invisible resisting force halted him. As swiftly as his thought had started him upon his meteoric course, this same unknown, unexplainable impulse bore him down once more 'till the earth loomed large below.

He readily yielded to this mysterious power; indeed, felt it would be utterly hopeless to attempt resistance. Again, as if in answer to his thought, he sped on; this time guided by the unseen hand.

Had he known his destination, the mere willing of himself there would have meant instant arrival. As it was, urged on by this mysterious something, he rushed on with a speed mocked by the fastest airplane.

A wanderer from childhood, Joe Carson had been to the far corners of the earth and back again. The far reaches of the dark African jungle; India with its age-old mysticism; the desert sands of Arabia; the old world cities of Europe, he had seen them all. He was as much at home in a crude bamboo hut in the interior of Japan as he was in the most pretentious manor in England. It was out of this vast experience, this rubbing of elbows with the other peoples of the world, this mingling with the lesser understood races, that he had gleaned the knowledge which prompted this experiment---this adventure.

Perhaps this was the reason he felt no trepidation nor uneasiness over the uncertain terminal of his journey. Where-ever he should chance to come to earth he felt that he would find a spot with which he was fairly familiar.

On, ever on, into the night!

But was it night? He became conscious of a faint brightness spreading over the universe, increasing in brilliancy as he traveled on.

All at once he felt his headlong flight checked. The same guiding impulse manifested itself once more, this time drawing him to the world below. A tingling of elation swept through him. At last he had reached the end of his journey!

As he came closer to the earth, the objects began to take on some semblance of definite shape. The rugged contour of the hills, the shimmering blue of the water as the morning sun shone down upon it, the long stretches of lowlands between the hills all seemed like old friends.

He wished to be down where he could see to what clime his impulse had brought him. With the thought he found himself but a few hundred feet above the scene.

A single glance sufficed to bring a reminiscent. wave upon him. Campania! He wondered what errant prompting had brought him here. He thought of the delightful hours he had whiled away upon its sunny shores. His eyes swept the beautiful scene with a flash of recognition for each landmark that came within his range of vision.

The delicate curves of the drowsy mountains with their snowy peaks blended harmoniously in the opalescent distance. In the hazy vista the cloud-capped peaks of Abruzzi rose above the horizon, and the mountains of Sorrento bowed to the sea. He turned his glances to the north where the gloomy bulk of Vesuvius itself, from which a long trial of smoke curled upward.

Again he pondered as to why this peaceful place had been chosen for his destination. As if in reply, he found himself gently moving toward the slumbering mount of death and destruction.

He had heard many strange tales in the hours he had spent in the shadows of this mountain. Stories of the forgotten days when Sirens dwelt on the shores of the Tyrrhenian Sea; weird tales of Circe, of Scylla and Charbdis; of days when this wonder spot had been the favored seat of Venus until the forces of evil had overthrown her and destroyed the city which had been her special charge.

He drifted over Somma, floated across the deep, sickle-shaped valley that separated it from its sister peak, and finally hovered over the huge funnel-like crater of the old mountain itself.

He wondered after all if the legends were so absurd as they had seemed. The mountain appeared to be a living, pulsating being; weird, eerie, uncanny. It lured him, fascinated him, beckoned him to its warm bosom which as if the fabled temptress of old had taken possession for a time of this old, historical place and was leading him on to his destruction.

The hallucination grew in its intensity. Forgotten

were all his thought of occult theories. He felt himself drawn into the volcano's maw!

Under the spell of this same mystical influence, he fancied that the mighty jaws of the mountain opened wider to receive him, as he passed on into the vast elliptical chasm. Grotesque, ghastly shadows danced before him on the precipitous, fissured inner walls. Nearer and nearer to the fiery pit of the old crater until, forgetting that he was but a disembodied spirit, forgetting that things material could do him no physical harm Joe Carson made an ineffectual struggle against the forces that were drawing him down!

A moment more and he would plunge straight into the molten mass below. A queer idea flashed into his mind. Perhaps he was dead! Perhaps it was Mephistopheles who was calling him to the very depths of Inferno!

Even as he speculated the unseen power that guided him checked his course once more, he found himself drifting toward a cavernous fissure in the right wall---straight through the opening---into the side of the volcano!

Then, in the Stygian blackness that engulfed him, he felt his speed suddenly accelerated. Faster, ever faster, he flew. Down, down, and still down---as though his destination must be the innermost bowels of the earth! Was he a modern Aenaes and this his cavern of the Sibyl? Would he, too, find himself at last in the realm of the shadows?

CHAPTER IV
VESUVIA

All sense of direction, all reckoning of time and distance was lost as he catapulted on through the vast void. The heavy blackness wrapped itself about him like a thick mantle. He longed for just one ray of cheering light to penetrate the encompassing gloom.

After a time his terror abated and he regained much of his self-possession. He had staked all on this venture, had placed himself in the hands of destiny; very well, then, he would let said Destiny have a free hand. He began to look forward with eager anticipation to what awaited him at his journey's end.

At last the Cimmerian gloom seemed to lighten. The inky blackness became infused with the soft gray of purpling twilight. Then, in the far distance, a pin-point of light appeared.

His already terrific speed was doubled. So fast was he traveling that it seemed he remained motionless while the ever widening ray bore down upon him with his own tremendous speed. A final spurt, a flood of light, and he came to an abrupt stop. Swaying idly, he scanned the scene and took note of his surroundings.

A colossal cliff loomed behind him, dotted with the mouths of many caves, some of them hundreds of feet from the ground. Its sheer, perpendicular side stretched up until it seemed to meet the cloudless sky. He decided that he must have emerged from one of the many caverns, though which one it was impossible to determine.

At the base of the cliff lay a vast jungle of giant trees trees intertwined in a titanic arbor. Thick foliage hid the earth below. Straight ahead, miles wide, this ribbon of tangled tree-tops stretched out in an unbroken line. Far off to the left the landscape was screened by a misty veil of flame-flecked white that surged and pulsated like a thing alive. At his right, dimly outlined in the distance, rose the irregular oval walls of an ancient city.

The whole scene was bathed in an effulgence that Carson could liken only to his own sky as it is sometimes lighted by the reflection of a distant conflagration. His eyes vainly swept the cloudless vault above for some trace of sun, moon, stars. It was awesome; yet magnificent in its awesome-ness---as though the velvet dome of this inner world had caught and held the brilliance of a blazing sphere---a radiance that tinted the leaves of the monster trees with marvellous hues.

Once more came the feeling of lethargy that had possessed him as he hovered over the city at the start of his journey. This time, however, came no prompting of the unseen force which had led him to this wonderland. Subconsciously he knew that he had reached his goal. He wondered what lay hidden beneath the screening trees, but some sixth sense warned against choosing the heart of the wilderness for his experiment. The walled city at the right seemed to beckon him .

He floated lazily over the treetops trying to penetrate the dense foliage and see what lay below. Once he thought he heard the whirring of mammoth wings but laid it to imagination when the sound was not repeated.

He must have travelled a dozen miles in this manner, yet the city seemed as distant as when he started. He wondered if it were only a mirage; then dismissed the thought as asinine. He would soon find out. He willed himself to the edge of the jungle and paused again to study the new vista which lay before him.

For perhaps a mile from the edge of the jungle stretched a verdant tableland. This gave way to a gradual elevation leading to a wide plateau where stood the city he had seen from afar. The oval wall which encompassed it was all of fifty feet high and in a state of preservation which led him to hope he would find it abandoned despite its apparent antiquity. At intervals along the wall, square towers projected above it, each several stories high. From his vantage-point he could see a gateway directly ahead; a large, arched opening that reached nearly to the top of the protecting wall. At either side of this central gateway was a lateral entrance about half as high and wide. On the left of the archway, outside the walls, a colossal statue mounted on a pedestal stood guard. Bathed in the eerie light of this strange world it seemed sinister and foreboding. He hoped it was not indicative of the race he would find peopling this centuried city. For, even at this distance, he recognized it as a gigantic Hermanubis—the body of a Hercules and the head of a dog!

He shuddered at the thought. Then he remembered that he was still immune from any dangers the place might hold. Until he had summoned his physical self to join him he was free to will himself instantaneously to some more favorable spot. But was he? He had not forgotten the unknown force which had drawn him to this undiscovered land. Curiosity prompted him to further explorations. Another moment and he hovered above the city.

At the height of the elevation, at almost the exact center of the place, a square of Doric columns reared against the sky; half the height of the grayish walls and a good four feet in diameter. Above this colonnade was a gallery. The open central area was paved with slabs of the same grayish rock which formed the walls. In front of the columns and porticoes stood pedestals bearing statues, with the frightful Anubis holding a place of honor. Except for the odd statues the scene touched a chord in Carson's memory. Suddenly it came to him, and he thrilled with the elation of a mighty discovery.

Swiftly his eyes swept the rest of the scene in confirmation of his wild imaginings. The narrow, rutted streets, with their side footways and foot-high curbs; the low houses with their over-hanging balconies; the Corinthian and Doric architecture of the larger buildings. He could not be wrong; yet it seemed impossible that he could be right! Here, in the heart of the earth, beneath the very mountain that had caused its destruction was Pompeii! But a Pompeii such as not even the most enthusiastic archeologist had ever pictured in his wildest dreams!

If this was true he need no longer fear the suggestion which lurked in the terrifying statues. His mind went back to the days he had spent in the Dead City of the outer would. The religion of the ancients had always interested him and he had listened intently to all the tidbits of gossip he could pick up while he studied the ruins of the age-old places of worship. He remembered particularly the Temple of Isis, which was not a *templum* at all, but an *aedes*; perhaps because he was impressed with the idea of finding a breath of Egypt in such a purely Roman setting, perhaps because he had learned that the worship of this goddess of the Nile had been forbidden by decree of the Roman Senate, yet flourished despite the official ban.

He dropped closer to the earth, before the gray columns of the Forum to better study the statues. Yes, there was Isis herself, holding a bronze sistrum; there, too, the silent Orus, finger on lips enjoining reverent silence on the worshippers; Bacchus; the ox, Apis; and strange, uncouth images which seemed to couple the mysteries of Egyptian idolatry with that of voluptuous Rome. A recreated Pompeii though it might be—and was so far as physical aspect was concerned---these statues gave ample proof that he was in a modern Isiaca.

He fell to speculating as to what manner of people these Vesuvians might be. How had they come there? How was it he found in the bowels of the earth a city of which the buried one above was only a tiny replica? Which had come first? Had the Pompeii he knew been built by pioneers from the subterranean land who had found a way into the outer world in the dim ages of the Dead City's beginning? Was this the reason that historians and etymologists could not penetrate the veil of its earlier days, before it was occupied by the Etruscans? Or had the followers of the goddess, incensed by the ruling against them, led by some of the more resolute priests, migrated to the heart of the universe and founded this inner land where all would be free to pay homage to their chosen saint? And why, if either of these explanations proved to be the true one, had the city remained untouched by the march of progress? Would he find the customs of this new-old land paralleled those of the civilization our scientists had pictured from their knowledge of ancient Rome as the inscriptions in the buried city were slowly excavated? Or would he find some new and terrible things that would fill the stoutest heart with quaking fear?

He stopped short in his reverie. As yet he had had no evidence that this city was peopled. All that lay before him were silent buildings of grayish stone, deserted streets and inarticulate walls.

Then he saw that which made his senses quicken; that which convinced him that whatever the dangers of this inner world, here was the place where he would attempt his transmutation. Then he knew what the unseen force had been which had drawn him here; the call of soul to soul!

There, at the feet of Isis---that he had taken only for a whiter patch of stone in the pedestal---knelt a girl in an attitude of devout supplication. Her long black hair flowed over her bare shoulders and across her spotless low-cut tunic. Her skin was the color of a ripe olive. The uncanny light stamped her face with a rare, ethereal beauty. To Carson she, too, seemed a Goddess; one he would far rather worship than the cold stone to which she offered her prayers!

CHAPTER V
ALETHEA

Joe Carson hardly knew what drew his attention from

the scene, but he turned his glance a bit to the left just in time to see a brawny masculine form emerge from behind one of the huge columns and steal silently toward the kneeling girl.

His first feeling was one of deep chagrin that he had allowed himself to be so carried away by the mere sight of this unknown worshipper. After all he simply interrupted a tryst between some olive-skinned Juliet and her latest Romeo! He was about to turn away, to drift over the rest of the city, but that same mystic force halted him. He chafed at the resistance but that momentary delay determined his whole future course of action.

Now the man was but a few paces from the girl. For the first time, Carson realized that she was unaware of the newcomer's approach, that she was still wrapped in her silent devotions. A moment more and his shadow loomed large against the gray of the pedestal.

Warned by some subtle sense, the girl lifted her eyes. Silently she sprang to her feet with the lightness of a frightened doe and swung around to face the man.

Carson dropped to the level of the street, within arm's length of the pair. The man was breathing heavily, his face livid with bestial sensuality. The girl's lips were pressed tightly together, her eyes filled with sudden recognition and fear.

Another step and his coarse fingers gripped her bare shoulder. With a sudden lunge she slipped from his grasp, but with a bound he was on her again; one hand clutching her long hair with a force that snapped her head back painfully, while the other clawed at her loose tunic and with a mighty pull ripped it to shreds.

But it was not until he crushed her lithe young body in his huge arms that Carson roused himself from the lethargy which had held him spellbound. At last he knew that the moment had come to complete his transmutation. With all the latent power of his will he summoned his body to join him.

For one awful moment, Joe Carson thought he would fail. Then he felt the cold earth under his feet and knew that the experiment was not attempted in vain.

In the struggle, the pair had swung around so that the man faced Carson. The latter could see the Vesuvians's eyes dilate as he materialized from thin air. As Carson sprang for him, he flung the girl to the ground and waited to meet him with outstretched arms.

Carson checked his impetuous attack just in time. Strong though he was, and used to all kinds of rough and ready fighting, Carson knew he would be no match for those gorilla-like arms. Science rather than brute force must win this fight if he was to be the victor. He ducked as the other's arms closed over empty air, and swung with all his might for the point of the antagonist's jaw.

The blow caught the man flush on the point of the chin. A less powerful brute would have been down for the count. As it was, he swayed dizzily, spun around in a half-circle, regained his footing, and came at Carson once more.

A moment of fighting and Carson was convinced that the Vesuvian knew nothing whatever of boxing. Once those talon-like fingers half-closed about Carson's shoulder and he winced at the pain. Subconsciously he marveled at the bravery of the girl to keep from crying aloud when those same fingers had seized her, and at her unsuspected strength in being able to wrench herself free. He knew that once those fingers found the grip they were seeking that his adversary could break him as easily as a boy snaps a twig. Carson's only salvation lay in systematically and scientifically wearing him down 'till one of his punches to the unguarded jaw would have the desired effect.

He rained blow after blow to the man's face 'till it was little more than a gory mass of shredded skin, but still the man fought on. Carson felt himself losing ground; it was not human for anyone to stand up under such punishment as he was inflicting. He was beginning to tire from the strain. He gauged the distance to that iron jaw and drew back his fist for a final blow, calling on every muscle in his body to aid its effectiveness.

But the blow never landed. A dull thud, the sickening sound of shattered bones, and the body of Vesuvian dropped an inert mass on the paving stones at his feet.

Carson had forgotten the girl. Now he glanced up at where she stood above the still form of his adversary. In her hands she held a small statue of Anubis which she had wrested from its pedestal. Her bosom was heaving from her exertions and her bare breasts were spattered with blood from the skull of the man at her feet. She would have brought the image down upon the silent man for a finishing blow, but Carson caught her eye and motioned for her to leave him alone.

For a second the girl hesitated. Then she flashed Carson a smile and silently returned the blood-stained idol to its accustomed place. In a moment she was back with him, and after a cautious glance in all directions, still silent, she grasped his hand and indicated by a gesture that he should come with her.

Together they sped through the deserted streets until she paused before one of the stone houses. With another look about to satisfy herself that they were not observed, she pushed open the double doors and motioned Carson inside. As she followed and shut down the bolt with what he thought was undue haste, for the second time it seemed to him that he could hear the sinister whirring of giant wings---only this time it seemed louder, closer than before!

They stood in the spacious hallway for a moment and the girl signaled for Carson to wait by the door. He nodded assent and watched her disappear into one of the alcoves at the right of the atrium.

As he waited, his ears pressed close to the door to catch the slightest sound of pursuers or that eerie flapping of wings, he wondered with what strange manner of people he had chosen to ally himself. A girl whose exotic beauty would win her a place in the foremost ranks of stage or screen in the world he had left behind; a man whose sheer brute force would put to shame the strongest man our earth might match against him. And yet something about them struck him as being extremely odd. He racked his brain for the solution. He had it ! From the moment the girl had sprung, terror-stricken, to her feet; all the while she struggled in the man's powerful arms; even when he had appeared before them from the ether, and through the ensuing battle; neither of them had uttered so much as a single sound! Even after the man lay limp at his feet the girl had spoken only by signs! Could it be that he had stumbled into a land of mutes? What else could explain the uncanny silence that surrounded the city? Where were the other inhabitants? Were this man and girl the sole survivors of a race which had long since ceased to live upon his earth?

No! At least his last guess was wrong. She was returning, and with her came a gray-bearded man as big and brawny as the one from whom they had fled! A white toga covered his heavy frame, but the knotted muscles on his bare arms and legs caused Carson's eyes to bulge in frank amazement. A glance at his face, and Carson knew from the marked resemblance that this must be the father of the girl. With such a parent there was little need to wonder at the strength and stamina she had displayed!

Again he was wrong! If the girl was typical of this unknown race they were far from being dumb! Words were tumbling from her lips as fast as she could speak them while her companion listened intently. They were too far away for him to catch the words, for her voice was lowered almost to a whisper but Carson knew that he was the subject of the discourse for the man's eyes sought the door and rested upon him.

As they drew nearer, the girl stopped talking, and the man struck his hands together sharply. Before the echo had died away, a distinctive black, naked except for a loin cloth, stood at his elbow. He spoke sharply to him in a tongue that was totally unfamiliar, and the slave scurried away. Then he beckoned Carson to join them where they waited at the edge of the marble basin that filled the center of the court.

Carson ventured a nod as he approached them, and, the girl flashed an answering smile. The man's stern face remained unchanged and he greeted Carson in a monosyllabic guttural which seemed to be made up entirely of consonant sounds.

The occultist shook his head and spoke to the man in English. A puzzled look crossed his features and he answered in a still different dialect, though one equally unintelligible. Carson marveled at his linguistic ability.

The girl touched her father's shoulder and they interchanged meaning glances. He answered her unspoken question and Carson thrilled at the thought that after all he would be able to talk to them; not fluently, at first, perhaps, but enough so that he could make himself understood! For the language the man used in addressing the girl was the pure Roman of Caesar's day! Carson followed his words closely.

"No, Alethea, he is not one of the white priest of Bubon. Neither is he one of the fabled race which lives beyond the waters of flame. A stranger he must be, else never would he have had the temerity to attack one of the purple toga; a stranger, else would he have feared to be about after the hours of light had passed. Go now to your room, child, the excitement must have wearied you. Sleep, for you must be fresh to face the coming of a new day. The death of Ramanum will not be easily dismissed by his royal uncle, and never yet has one of the house of Maestro feared to face the wrath of Romulo! Sleep, and I will try to learn more of this stranger who has saved my house from dishonor and who I believe comes as a friend. "

"But, father - - -"

"Go, Alethea! Since when has a daughter of the white togas earned the right to question her parent's word?

Carson was on the point of protesting, of asking that the girl might remain, but something made him refrain as she turned her back and headed for her room. The slave had returned bringing a toga, spotless as the one which his involuntary host wore. Carson felt himself burn from head to toe. So strenuous had been the battle in the streets, so mysterious the flight to the house, so interesting the brief moments he had spent with the pair, that 'till this very moment he had been entirely unconscious of one thing. The first state of the experiment had succeeded beyond his fondest dreams. He had drawn his body by the sheer power of will into the very bowels of the earth. But he had left his clothes behind!

Had he but known what he learned in the next few days, Carson would have realized the mark of honor his host conferred in offering him the toga. Clothes in this subterranean land were the exception rather than the rule. Three classes alone were garbed: those of the royal family; the people of the temple; and the counselors, to whom in times of stress both throne and temple turned. The populace at large, of both sexes, wore merely a cloth about the loins, its color and richness of design dependent upon the social and financial status of the individual in the community.

He slipped into the garment the black held for him. Then, haltingly, he addressed the master of the house in his own tongue! For the first time, he favored Carson with a smile and bade him follow.

He led the way across the spacious tablinum through a narrow corridor at the right to the peristyle. Carson caught his breath at the sheer beauty of the scene---the stately columns on all sides with their connecting balustrades, the sculptured fountain in the center, the garden at the rear with its wealth of rare, exotic blooms.

Carson guessed where they were bound even before the host swung into the right wing---the triclinium. The horse-shoe of triple beds had been made in readiness for them; a dining-room that smacked of Nero and the voluptuous orgies of Rome's most hectic days!

He wondered if age-old custom would be followed, and if so who the third party at the meal would be. His host clapped his hands once more and spoke again in the language of the black dwarf who answered the summons. Carson could understand but one word of it---Alethea---the name by which the man had called his daughter. Perhaps he had changed his mind and decided to call her into conference after all. Carson hoped so!

Roman in speech, Roman in architecture, Roman in custom! At least their names were far from Roman either in sound or construction. Carson mentally repeated the names he had already heard mentioned by the man at his side:

"Bubon . . . . . Romanum . . . . . Romulo . . . . . Maestro . . . . . Alethea---"

He found himself saying that last name over and over as the servants made ready for the meal. Alethea! What a name to conjure with---and what a girl.

CHAPTER VI
REVELATIONS AND RIDDLES

It was not Alethea who joined them, however, but a stalwart youth whom Carson guessed to be about two years the girl's senior. His resemblance to man and maid was so striking that Carson was not surprised when Maestro introduced him as his son, Ornoco.

First of all, Carson explained to the best of his ability how and why he had come to their land. He could see incredulity written on their faces, particularly that of the younger man, as he tried to convey the idea of bodily transmutation through space. To convince them, he staged a brief demonstration similar to that which he had offered before the society. At its conclusion, Maestro gripped his hand.

"Welcome, friend. Should you care to tarry in Vesuvia my house and its servants are yours to command."

Carson thanked him simply and reminded him that his stay was limited.

"But while I am here I wish to learn all that I can of your land and its people, that when I return I may have much of interest to tell my friends on the earth from whence I came.

Ornoco would have spoken, but his father checked him with upraised hand.

"It has been my life work to keep straight the history of our race. What little I have gleaned from the records of my predecessors I will be pleased to tell you, briefly. If time permits, you may have access to our archives.

"Our race, too, came from the earth you call your

home. Of necessity, our earlier history is vague and incomplete. Perhaps your own knowledge may supplement ours. Over sixteen centuries ago our ancestors were part of a great empire such as the world had never known. Their ruler was one Tibeo or Tibeum. Their city had not so long been rebuilt after a great catastrophe which had leveled their most beautiful structures. One of their temples was built near a huge hill of fire, and the disturbance which ruined their city had opened a large fissure in the earth beneath it that which our forefathers, priests of the temple, discovered.

"A handful of these daring men explored this tunnel and some believed it led to a land where they might find freedom in a religion which was frowned upon by their ruler. With some of the stout-hearted maidens of the temple, they threaded their way beneath the hill of fire to this inner world. From those brave few, has grown our present city of over twenty thousand.

"For centuries they battled against unequal odds, at last subduing the black dwarfs who peopled the vast forest and making them our slaves. But not 'till two centuries ago did we suspect that our little world extended beyond the River of Flame at the end of the Dark Forest.

"Then came the Bubons, and with them the end of our hard-earned freedom. For fifty years our history is one of appalling carnage until at last a truce was effected---a victory that in itself spelt defeat and bondage .

"During the hours of light we are free to do as we choose, but we are forbidden by royal edict to be upon the streets after the time of darkness begins. Vainly have we sought to discover the passage leading to the outer world, and when you claimed it as your home I hoped you might be able to show us the way."

Carson queried as to what the punishment be; Ornoco shuddered, and Maestro grew grim once more.

"Had you cried aloud while you battled in the street, my friend, you would have had an answer to both your questions. There are but two things feared in Vesuvia---and one of these is the wrath of Romulo, which I fear tonight's adventure will draw down upon both my daughter and you. The other . . . . . " He shrugged his shoulders. "This is the Ides of August, and today began the eight-day Fete of Sanctity. It is for that, Alethea braved the hours of darkness to implore her goddess for special protection."

"And that other is . . . . . ?"

"It were better that I even banish the thought of it from my mind, lest the thought beget the actuality! Should the worst come, you will learn---and wish, perhaps, that you had not known!"

Carson switched his questioning. The Vesuvian day, he learned, is divided into two equal parts of fifteen hours each. There are neither sun, moon, nor stars. The source of light and its regulation is as much a mystery as it was the day the first intrepid explorers stepped foot in the subterranean world. There is neither dawn nor twilight---just an instantaneous change. One moment the land is flooded with a warm, radiant glow; the next it is dark but for the eerie reflection in the sky that reminds one of a distant, blazing city.

Their calendar conforms exactly to the Julian system except for the length of the days; that is, a Vesuvian year, while made up of the same number of weeks months and days as our own, is actually equivalent of a year and three months as we figure time. Carson had left the earth on February 18, 1930. He mentally calculated. If he were correct, then he had arrived at his destination on the Ides of August---1549!

All this while Carson was searching his brain to correlate if he could the history of his own world with the brief outline Maestro had given him. Here was the clue---the difference in time! The place, of course, was Pompeii; the emperor, Tibernius; the catastrophe, the earthquake of 63 B.C.! And the subsequent eruption of Vesuvius, which had wiped out the twin cities at its base, had closed the passageway to the outer world!

He put his thoughts into words, and the eyes of Maestro lighted with the enthusiastic fire one sees only in a zealot. The historian knew that could he supply the missing links in the early records of his people, even the Buboes could not keep him from the Vesuvian Hall of Fame.

He plied Carson with questions 'till the latter's meager store of knowledge was exhausted and Ornoco braved the fear of a reprimand by suggesting that perhaps the stranger would find sleep welcome. Maestro was all apologies for this thoughtlessness and a few moments later Carson was ensconced in a bed-chamber.

But sleep was long in coming. Question followed question in his overtired brain. Who was this Romanum whom he had left inert at his feet some hours before? What was the significance of the purple toga? Who was Romulo that he was to be so feared? What was the unutterable punishment for being found on the streets during the hours of darkness?

From what ancient race sprang these ebony pygmies who had become Vesuvian slaves? What were the Bubons? What danger did Alethea face that sent her out to the feet of her goddess where Carson had found her? What new trouble had he caused her by his impetuous interference?

Alethea! His tired brain seemed to find rest in painting a mental picture of the girl; the rare, ethereal beauty of her face as he had seen it in the weird night light of the city, the rich olive of her skin, her luxuriant, glossy-black hair.

CHAPTER VII
ROMULO DECREES

Joe Carson opened his eyes on a world that was bright with the brightness of noonday to find Ornoco at his bedside speaking his name.

"Though I hated to disturb your slumbers, my father thought you might wish to join us. We go to the court of Rumulo in another hour."

Romulo! The name had been associated with the girl the night before. Carson spoke her name aloud before he thought.

"Alethea! Your sister . . . . ."

Ornoco smiled.

"She is waiting for us to join her in the morning meal. It is true that she has been summoned to appear because of last night's experience, but I cannot see where she has broken any law."

"But the man we left lying upon the street . . . . ."

"Has long since met the fate of those who venture forth after the hours of light have passed."

"But your sister and I . . . . ."

The youth seemed determined not to let Carson complete the sentence.

"As long as you kept quiet you were comparatively safe. The darkness had just closed in about us. An hour later, not even your silence would have saved you."

"Then why has she been summoned?"

Ornoco could not mask his uneasiness.

"I do not know, my friend. That is why I am troubled."

A question had been in Carson's mind since the conversation had started. He took advantage of the other's silence to put it into words.

"Who is this Romulo, that even his name causes such visible distress?"

Ornoco flashed him a momentary glance of astonishment. Then he smiled.

"I had forgotten that you had been in our land but a night. Romulo, Emperor of Vesuvia, has spoken; and when Romulo speaks, Vesuvia trembles and obeys!"

He might have guessed it! Then the people of the purple toga must be members of the royal family. And the man Alethea had slain was a nephew of Romulo! Carson whistled softly.

By this time he had dressed and they made their way to where Maestro and his daughter waited. They greeted him affably, but Carson could sense some fear of unknown yet definite danger ahead. They ate in silence and Carson felt his host's eyes upon him several times during the meal, as though trying to read his thoughts.

It would have been a job for a psychologist of the highest order. They were chaotic to the Nth degree. Carson doubted very much if he could have expressed them coherently had his host inquired.

It was not until the last dish had been removed that Maestro broke the ominous quiet.

"Ornoco has told you?"

"Only that your daughter must go before the Emperor because of what occurred last night, and that you wish me to go along."

"I cannot guess what lies behind the summons, but our uncertainty will soon be allayed. I hoped that you would go, too, that Romulo might meet the stranger from the world above. Better that you go to him than that he hear of your presence and summon you!"

"I come from a land where empires are fast becoming democracies. I fear your Romulo less than . . . . ."

Alethea gasped in sudden terror, and Maestro checked Carson with a gesture.

"It is well that you are among friends, else you would feel already a taste of his power! Even so, it is better to let such thoughts remain unspoken. Traitors and spies there are in every household."

Carson nodded.

"I will gladly go, on one condition."

"And that is?"

"That I be allowed to tell of my part in the affair. Your

daughter should not be made to bear the brunt of his wrath. I am as much to blame as she."

Alethea made as if to protest but her father caught her eye. He rose and crossed to Carson, placed a hand on his shoulder, and looked full into his eyes.

"Well spoken, my new found friend! You shall have your opportunity, though I fear that you will be unable to moderate whatever punishment may be meted out to her. Come, we must be on our way. I had hoped today to be able to entertain you in a manner fitting to so unusual a guest. Perhaps after this is through there will yet be opportunity."

They stepped out into the street and for a moment it seemed to Carson that while he slept he had been transported to another land. The world was ablaze with a brilliance which seemed to come from every point of the compass and fuse into a sea of soft, warm rays. The streets that had been deserted when he hovered above the city, now swarmed with people. Naked children trailed at the heels of olive-skinned women clad only in the loin cloths of the commoners; undersized blacks scurried to and fro jostling elbows with men and women in wraps of white, purple and saffron. Purple, Carson had learned, meant the members of the court; white, he guessed, belonged to the sages; he wondered now at the significance of the yellow. He was soon to learn!

They threaded their way through the throng to their destination. Carson was conscious of the glances that were cast his way. He was of an alien race; yet he was robed in the white of the academicians and many of those who eyed him askance nodded affably to his companions.

Carson felt an eerie sense of unreality sweep over

him. It almost seemed that all this was but a weird dream, an atavistic phantasy. He, Joe Carson, a strictly twentieth century product, born and bred in a world that was thrilling to one new scientific discovery after another, was living and breathing and walking the streets in a land where, to all outward appearances, civilization had not progressed since Nero's day!

It was impossible---yet it must be so! These people with whom he mingled as he followed his guides were as real, as surely creatures of flesh and blood as he. For instance, there was Alethea. Strange how he could not keep his eyes from her when there was so much else to be seen! If dream this was, and she a part of it, Carson yearned to dream on forever!

But that tug at his elbow was material enough. It was Ornoco.

"This way, my friend. Here is the court of Romulo."

Carson was a bit disappointed. He had expected to find a ruler so feared as this one holding court in a palace which would put the Caesars' to shame. Instead, he followed the trio into a plain, long hall---immensely long! The interior was severely free from anything in the way of pomp or beauty. Along the walls on either side, clear to the edge of the dais at the further end, Carson had marveled only a few short hours before at the prowess and stamina of the girl who was leading the way. He marveled still more at the Amazonic army who bore the shields and the spears. Immobile as carven statues the tensed muscles stood out on their nude torsos like wavelets in a rippling stream. Girls such as these could make even blase Broadway bow!

But Joe Carson lost interest in the guardians of the court as he neared the throne of the man who made Vesuvia tremble. As he glimpsed the misshapen form which occupied the throne, it was all he could do to keep from shrieking aloud with ill-timed laughter. But, as he looked, Carson's desire to laugh waned.

He was scarcely taller than the Nubians who served him; his shoulders hunched so high that his body seemed neckless; his short legs dangled grotesquely halfway to the floor; two unmatched eyes leered malevolently over a gigantic nose; this mouth was just a wide slit above a sharply receding chin. More a gnome, than a man, a gargoyle born not of woman but cast from some forgotten mold in the foundries of Nastrond! His toga of royal purple accentuated the impression of Evil, concentrated and personified---Evil that held supreme power in the hollow of its hand!

As if in contrast, a yellow-robed figure, straight and towering, stood beside the regent's chair. He watched with impassive eyes as the quartette halted before Romulo's throne. One gained the impression that his mind wrested with problems far more urgent than the hearing of this girl who made obeisance before them.

Romulo waved the girl to her feet. With the same motion, his long arm swept round to include the saffron-clad companion. The slit that formed his mouth yawned wide, and from it issued a sound more like the roar of a frenzied beast than human speech, a sound that filled every inch of the spacious court, and threatened to wreck the walls with its reverberations.

"Alethea, daughter of Maestro, I have summoned you

to answer grave charges brought against you by Bunos."

At the mention of his name the man in the yellow robes bowed ever so slightly, and Alethea's eyes lighted with sudden fear.

Carson flashed an inquisitive glance at Ornoco, and strained his ears to catch the whispered reply.

"Bunos, High Priest of the Temple, whose power is second only to Romulo!"

So the yellow garb stood for the sanctified! He should have known. But the emperor's voice was booming again. What was this heinous crime the girl had committed?

Bunos reports that a statue of Anubis has been defiled with human blood. The paving stones nearby were splotched with red, and almost at the feet of Isis herself was found the remnants of a tunic of white. Bunos has examined this and brought it to me for confirmation. As is the custom throughout Vesuvia among those who are entitled by rank to wear a tunic or toga, each garment must be marked with the insignia of the family to which the owner of the garment belongs. The torn cloth which Bunos has brought me is stamped unmistakably with the mark of Maestro. And you, Alethea, have neither mother nor sister!"

Alethea drew herself to her full height. Her eyes flashed, her voice was firm and clear.

"Romulo, in his wisdom, has drawn the logical and the obvious conclusion. It was in the first hour of darkness. The blood is that of one who sought to bring dishonor to her who wore the white robe the mouthpiece of Isis has found. Small wonder Bunos counts as a desecration the blood of one whose thoughts were so unclean!"

Carson thrilled anew at the hardihood of the girl to speak in such a manner to the uncle of the man she had slain. He wondered if Romulo knew the identity of the victim.

Romulo's mismated eyes twinkled as they met those of the priest in a brief glance of understanding. They grew stern once more as he addressed the girl.

"No one lives who dares accuse Romulo of injustice! I am disposed to be lenient, but the decision rests not with me. A sin against the Temple is not a crime against the Throne. Your fate is in Bunos' hands. It is only within my province to sentence you as he may decide."

What farce! What mockery! This loathsome, malignant thing upon the throne dared to prate of compassion when his whole demeanor bespoke putrid hate and venomous revenge. This was no sincere plea for clemency, but a carefully rehearsed plan to legitimately wreak his rancor upon this defenseless girl.

Carson remembered the promise he had exacted from Maestro, that he be permitted to bear his share of the blame. He had sensed a vague murmuring behind him as Romulo was speaking and now, as if in answer to his thought, Ornoco nudged him. Once more he listened closely to catch the whispered words.

"My father wishes that you keep silent. To speak means that you must share the penalty. Your chance to help Alethea will be greater if you keep your liberty. Alethea will understand. "

Carson acquiesced with a brief nod. Father and brother, too, had grasped the travesty of the proceedings. All eyes turned toward the tall priest as the emperor waited his pretended decision.

The Holy One's eyes still stared straight ahead, looking directly at the girl, yet as unconscious of her presence as though the hall was deserted. At last he spoke, and his voice was like that of some long-dead thing---toneless, lifeless, mechanical.

"The code of the Temple demands atonement from all who defile or debase it. Romulo, in all his wisdom, knows full well the laws of the Temple and the punishment provided for the offender. Isis frowns upon violence however great the provocation!"

The assorted eyes of the ruler danced in mephistic glee as they fastened for the last time on those of the girl.

"Bunos has spoken. Tomorrow falls the Tournament of the Unsanctified. You shall take your place among the gladiators. Bloodshed shall be expiated by bloodshed. I Romulo, Emperor of Vesuvia, have spoken!"

Once more his long arm waved. Two black pygmies appeared from behind the dais and stripped the garments from the girl, who had received her sentence with majestic stoicism. Six of the Amazonic guards came to sudden life and action and formed a circle about her, their spear-points touching her body from all sides. A final wave of the Emperor's arm and the sextette fell into step with their prisoner. Another moment and Alethea had vanished through a door at the right of the throne.

CHAPTER VIII
THUMBS DOWN!

Joe Carson could never more than vaguely remember what immediately followed the exit of this fearless girl. She had gone without so much as a parting glance toward the trio who had accompanied her. Maestro had said Alethea would understand his silence after the promise he had made. He wondered if she had understood, or if she had labeled him a coward, a craven, if that was why she had left them without the slightest sign she was aware that he existed.

He was dimly conscious that Maestro was presenting him to the Emperor and explaining his presence in their land. He had a hazy impression that Romulo's variegated orbs were burning into his own, that the thundering voice was mouthing congratulatory phrases and predicting new honors for the house of Maestro. At last it was over, and Carson stumbled blindly through the still crowded streets until he reached the sanctuary of the historian's home.

Maestro evidently divined his guest's mood. For more than an hour he left Carson to his own devices. Then, without so much as a reference either to the affair of the night before or the more recent calamitous happening, he excused himself on the plea of urgent research work and told Ornoco to see that Carson was adequately entertained.

Joe Carson wondered how much of Maestro's callousness was assumed. It seemed unnatural for a father to show so little concern in the fate of his only daughter. Perhaps this talk of work was only a blind and he was going to Alethea to explain, to comfort her. Carson could keep silent no longer. Ornoco tried to evade his queries but at last Carson wrung this meager information from him.

Maestro had not gone to Alethea for the all sufficient reason that visitors were absolutely forbidden to the gladiators who took part in the Tournament of the Unsanctified. To break this rule meant death to the guard who lapsed her vigilance, and life was not held so lightly in Vesuvia, despite the carnage in its fetes and spectacles. The probability was that Alethea was confined in the gladiator's quarters, adjoining the coliseum, where even now the preliminary sports and games of the Fete of Sanctity were being held. There she would stay 'till the morrow, when she would take her place in the arena to slay or be slain. One, and only one, of the score or more of temple violators would return to her people. That one, purged of her sin by the blood shed in mortal combat would take her place among the heroines of Vesuvia 'till the next gladiatorial queen was crowned. As for those who were defeated, Romulo held their lives in the hollow of his hand.

"If you wish, my friend," Ornoco concluded, "we can go now to the games as we had planned were Alethea still here."

"I hardly think so, Ornoco. I think I'll lie down for a while. I've been under quite a strain and I feel I need the rest. If I should want to stroll that way, later, alone, how do I get to the games?"

"I would be pleased to guide you, but if you should choose to go by yourself you should have no trouble. During the Fete of Sanctity all Vesuvia turns to the festivities. Just follow the throng beyond the court of Romulo to the edge of the city. Meanwhile, your room shall be at your disposal and I shall order Gogi to see that you are not disturbed."

Carson turned his head so that Ornoco would not see the odd gleam in his eyes. Thanking the youth, he made his way to his room, his step light, his brain athrob with the idea which had come to him. He would go to Alethea; he would see her; he would speak with her---yet he would remain unseen!

He stretched full length upon the bed, closed his eyes, and a moment later his ethereal ego soared above the court of Romulo.

Ornoco had said that all Vesuvia would be headed for the games. Joe Carson hovered above the crowded streets and watched the surging throng. The majority were wending their way slowly but surely past the court of the Emperor toward the outskirts of the city. Carson, as he sped along, above them, fell to wondering whimsically what they would say if they knew that he was there. It was only a matter of moments before he came in sight of the huge amphitheatre. Another moment and he looked down upon the arena, a sanded oval some seventy feet long and half as wide. His eyes swept over the twenty-four ranges of seats, already half filled with eager spectators.

He cast about for some inkling as to where he would find the gladiator's barracks. At one end of the amphitheatre, an arched doorway opened into a spacious cloister surrounded by pillars. Two of the Amazonic soldiers patrolled the entrance.

Prompted by that same intangible force which had already drawn him to Vesuvia, he willed his astral self inside. There he found half a hundred curious dwellings; crude, inhospitable. Undoubtedly these were the prisons. He hovered above them then, to test his conjecture, projected himself within the nearest one.

The girl confined there seemed to sense an alien presence. She was lying on the floor, back to him, and he watched as she tried to roll over in his direction; watched and marveled at the efficiency of the crude device which held her prisoner. It looked more like a prostate ladder than anything else he could think of---a ladder with four rungs between which the legs of the girl were clamped in such a way that she could neither rise nor turn. Her arms were fastened behind her with a similar ladder-like manacle. That was all, yet she was fastened securely enough to trouble a Houdini.

As he watched, Carson realized that the contour of the girl was oddly familiar. Once more he had been led inexorably to his goal. He whispered just loud enough for the recumbent girl to hear.

"Alethea."

Back came the voice he longed to hear; couched, too, in barely audible tones.

"Who are you? How came you here?"

"Joe Carson. You cannot see me, my physical body is in my room in your father's home. I came to see you, to talk with you, to see if there is any way that I can help you."

"I understand. Father told me of your powers that you demonstrated for him and for Ornoco. There is little you can do to aid me. Even were you to transport your physical self here, I fear these fastenings would baffle you---and even should you release me, I do not think I should care to flee. The daughter of Maestro fears not to face whatever the morrow may hold!"

"It is the thought that perhaps you might feel that I feared to speak as I promised, before Romulo, that brought me here."

"It is my wish, my friend. I talked it over with father on the way to court, and told him that if danger threatened me it was unwise that you, too, should be confined. Better that you retain your liberty, for who can tell what another day will bring? Already you have saved my honor, it may be that you can do still more.

"The sound of your voice has given me courage. The knowledge that I need not brave the coming ordeal alone steels me to stoic fortitude. Go, now, lest too much thought of the morrow might weaken my new found strength. Take with you the knowledge that I count you as more than merely a friend. I know that you care, and because I know I shall strive all the harder for victory."

A night had come and gone, a morning had dragged interminably by. At his request, Ornoco had ordered Gogi to serve his meals in his room. Maestro he had not seen 'till just prior to the time of their departure. Now at the side of Ornoco, he trailed the gray-haired historian through the crowded streets to the amphitheatre.

A few moments later, and the trio threaded their way through the throng to the seats in the lowest tier to which Maestro's rank entitled him .

Directly opposite, in his seat of State, was the odd-eyed monarch of the Vesuvians. His eerie eyes gleamed with eager anticipation of the spectacle about to be staged before him. At his side sat the yellow-clad Bunos, a sepulchral antithesis of the grotesque and misshapened Emperor.

A trumpet sounded. The carnage was about to begin. With an effort, Carson shifted his attention to the arena.

The ringmaster was tracing a circle in the sand with his long staff. Within this circle the gladiators must keep. The two maidens who were cast for the stellar roles in the first combat were already waiting at opposite sides of the circle. One of them, half armed, was blowing the trumpet, while two girls behind her held helmet and shield. Two slaves were bringing the other her helmet and sword.

The trumpets sounded again. The battle was on!

Carson marvelled at the adroitness with which the girls thrust and parried. Sword met sword or clanged sonorously against helmet or shield. A false move, and one sword buckled against the shield of the other. A lightning-like lunge and blood streamed down the arm of the luckless girl. Another, and her useless weapon dropped from her hand to the sand of the arena. The wounded arm stretched out toward the imperator, thumb raised.

He eyed her gloatingly for a full moment, then swept the circle of faces that looked down upon the scene. As if he read the answer in the few thumbs which pointed downward, Romulo turned his own thumbs down.

With measured stride the victor approached her late opponent. Her blood-stained sword curved upward-descended-and a lifeless body lay stretched upon the reddening sand.

An attendant appeared, a red-hot iron in hand. He pressed it deep into the flesh of the victim. The smell of searing skin assailed Carson's nostrils. It was nauseating---revolting! The body of the girl did not move, the victor had done her task well. A slave harpooned the body and dragged it through the mire of blood and sand to the narrow portal of death, where after being stripped of helmet and shield it would be flung into the spoiliarium.

Before the body had reached the gates, two more contestants were waiting.

This was to be a different version of the sport, evidently. One of them, as before, was armed with sword and helmet. The other bore in her left hand a three-pronged javelin, while in her right she carried a huge net. The blare of the trumpet urged them to action.

A moment or two and Carson caught the idea of this gamble with death. The girl with the net was seeking to throw it over the head of her adversary, while the latter was searching for an opening with her sword while keeping out of reach of the enmeshing folds. A sudden toss and the net descended to the shoulders of the helmeted girl, who fell on one knee and faced her fate. Once more the extended arm, thumb upraised. Once more the motion of the ruler which spelled her doom.

The victor's trident was not the right sort of weapon for dealing sure death. She caught up the sword the other had dropped, and as the condemned girl vainly clasped her knees, she rested one hand on the helmeted head and calmly slashed the throat of the one she had defeated.

Carson turned his face away. He had seen enough of this deliberate murder that seemed to thrill the occupants of the amphitheatre. He felt a tug at his toga. Ornoco pointed to the gate from which the gladiators entered. Carson felt a strange thrill tingle up and down his spine.

Alethea!

As she paused beneath his seat, she glanced up at him and smiled. She was still smiling as the slaves handed her the helmet, shield and sword. He glanced at the other girl. She was being similarly arrayed. Evidently this was to be a repetition of the first affray. At any rate, it gave Alethea a fighting chance.

The trumpet! The girls stepped into the circle of death. The sand beneath their feet was bright with the blood of the two who had fought and died. The combat was on!

Carson watched every pass of the cumbersome swords. In and out, up and down, they flashed and gleamed. Ah! A stream of red poured from the slashed side of Alethea's foe. But she still had her sword! From the rabble in the upper tiers came shouts to end the battle. Alethea spurred herself to a supreme effort. Her feet slipped in the slimy sand. A parry, and her sword was struck from her hand. She took time to smile up in Carson's direction. Then, calmly, she extended her arm.

Romulo's malevolent eyes swept the circle of faces. Hundreds of thumbs were turned up in a plea of mercy. The Emperor caught the High Priest's eye. As if by prearrangement, the latter shook his head. Audible groans and jeers came from the upper tiers as Romulo's thumbs turned down!

CHAPTER IX
AN ENVOY OF BUBO

Alethea's opponent stepped forward and swung her sword high in the air. The fated girl drew herself stiffly erect to meet the blow.

And then, over the rail of the arena to the bloody sand below, vaulted Joe Carson, stripping the white toga from him as he sped toward the pair. For the time being he was berserk. He lost sight of the fact that his feet had hardly touched the ground before attendants had started in his direction, forgot that it was a woman, like Alethea, he assailed. His one thought was that with the descent of that sharp sword Alethea's life would be ended, that her body would be branded with the red-hot iron of the slaves and her body dragged out of sight to the ignominious grave of a slaughtered gladiator.

He wrested the sword from the grasp of the startled girl whose duty it was to carry out her royal majesty's Ultimatum. Another moment and the sword dripped red, her body lay stretched upon the slimy sand.

The amphitheatre was in an uproar. From every side came cries of "Bravo" and "Mercy." Alethea was evidently a favorite among the Vesuvians, her champion a hero.

Now the attendants were upon him. Alethea had caught up her sword, and they stood back to back swinging their sharp weapons in death-dealing arcs around them.

Both man and girl were splashed with blood as the keen blades cut into the flesh of their foes. The arena was fast becoming a shambles. The odds were too great, slowly but surely the pair was forced back toward the wall of the arena. Carson guided their retreat so that as their backs at last touched the wall they were directly beneath Ornoco and the father of the girl. Forcing her behind him, hewing his way through yielding flesh and bone, he called to the men in the first tier, wondering if his voice would carry above the clashing of swords.

"Take the girl. Lift her out of the arena. Then I will surrender."

Willing hands reached down to do his bidding. He felt Alethea's body brush against his own as she was swung over the high wall. He fought wildly to keep any of the attendants from reaching her, pulling her down. Then, flinging his sword to one side, he stretched out his arm in the age-old sign.

Surrounded by his captors, he crossed the gore-stained sands and halted below the seat of Romulo.

The Emperor was on his feet, his mismatched eyes flaming with malevolence and hatred. Carson firmly expected him to order him spit upon the long javelins some of the attendants bore. But time-honored custom must at least be outwardly observed. The flashing eyes swept the amphitheatre. As if fearful that he would misinterpret the upraised thumbs which met his eyes, a thousand throats took up the cry: "Mercy! Mercy!" Even Nero in his most depraved debaucheries had more than once been forced to bow before this self-same cry.

But Romulo was not to be denied his revenge. Who was this white stranger who had violated every tradition of his sports and games, who had slain a score of his picked gladiators in hand-to-hand battle, who had snatched the girl he had marked for death from beneath his very nose? What cared he for the wishes of the multitude? Was not he Emperor of Vesuvius? Was not his word law? If they did not like his decision, they could complain to him at his court, next day. By then his desire would have been accomplished, his enemy removed. Let them howl!

Joe Carson could read his thoughts in those assorted eyes as readily as though Romulo had spoken them aloud. He knew that the crowd pleaded in vain with this hostile autocrat of an alien world. Romulo rose, and drew his grotesque body in what he thought was regal erectness. Slowly he shook his head in negation at the demands of the multitude.

And then, before the fateful signal could be given, a shadow crossed the sky above the arena. A moving shadow, a hurtling patch of mammoth darkness that caused every eye to be raised aloft. The voices ceased and a hushed silence fell over the amphitheatre. For the third time, Joe Carson heard the same sinister whirring of great wings that had marked his first day and night in this outre land.

The creature flew in narrowing circles above the center of the arena, each circle bringing it lower 'till he could nearly make out its shape with his naked eye. Then the wide wings closed, and its body hurtled earthward with plummet-like accuracy. A few feet from the ground its wings opened parachute-like, and it floated gently to the sands, wings that spread a full twenty feet from tip to tip.

An owl! And such an owl! Well over eight feet tall, a throat of pure white; its "vest" a dirty yellow, streaked with penciled bars! And such eyes, yellow eyes with dilating pupils whose disks threatened to hide the yellow background as it blinked in the unaccustomed light of day.

No wonder the Vesuvians feared the Bubons! Twice Rome underwent ceremonial purification because an owl had been found within the city. Before the death of the great Augustus an owl sang on the Curia, and the demise of both Valentinian and Commodus Antonius were presaged by owls lighting upon their homes. Though comrade and associate of Minerva, to the Roman mind the hollow hootings, the fearful shrieks and the serpent-like hissings of this ancient bird augured ill for all within the sound of its raucous voice.

The circle of gladiators had drawn back to a respectful distance, Carson still in the center. The bird advanced with mincing steps and bowed its hooded head before Romulo.

The Emperor addressed it, and Carson recognized the same monosyllabic guttural with which Maestro had first spoken to him.

Romulo's eyes gleamed oddly as they conversed. Carson happened to glance at Alethea and he noticed that her face was wan and drawn. What was the purpose of this visitation? How could it affect this girl he had twice saved from doom?

At last it was ended. Romulo, still standing, waved his hand. This time an absolute hush fell over the assemblage.

"Citizens and slave alike are aware that we are allowed our freedom only by sufferance of the Mighty Bubo. Absolute as is my power in my own domain, his is the greater. Once in a decade he exacts his toll. It is one of the conditions by which we are bound by our treaty.

"Let all assemble in the Forum at the fourth hour of

daylight tomorrow. It is mete that all honor be shown, meanwhile, to this distinguished envoy. By my royal edict the Fete of Sanctity, the Tournament of the Unsanctified, shall not be resumed until the second day."

He turned his attention to the coterie about Carson, and beckoned. As one they advanced to their former position before him.

"White stranger, in their foolish ardor, the people of my realm have asked that I be merciful. Tonight you shall go free to stop with the people of the girl you so rashly championed. Tomorrow I command that you be in the Forum and witness the ceremony, and that, in the sixth hour, you present yourself before me in my court that I may decide as to your penalty."

The emissary of the feathered tribe waited for his pronouncement to cease. Then, spreading his great wings, he rose above the tier of seats, and dropped lightly to a place at Romulo's side.

Carson, free, crossed the arena, and scrambled over the high wall to the side of the downcast girl.

CHAPTER X
HIGH PRIESTESS OF THE OWLS

Night. To the quartette in Maestro's home, the sudden closing in of darkness seemed to cast the shadow of impending tragedy upon the household. The afternoon had been given over to a discussion of the events at the amphitheatre and the probable consequences of Carson's impetuous act. Repeated reference had been made to the winged visitor and to the coming meeting in the Forum, but nothing had been said which would give Carson any tangible clue as to the part, if any, Aletha was to play. Yet, at every mention of the Bubon, he noticed her face went pale, and she struggled to suppress her emotions. It was not until the evening meal was through that he was able to steal a few moments alone with the troubled girl. Without preamble, he asked her pointblank the reason for her visible concern.

She looked long into his eyes as if to read the motive behind his question. When she spoke her voice was pregnant with pent-up passion.

"My friend---more than my friend---perhaps it is foolish to trouble you with my fears, which may after all be only spectral ones. Tonight, eight other girls in our land share my same feelings, yet the events of the past few hours lead me to believe that I, and I alone, have cause to be afraid.

"It was this fear which drove me into the streets the night you came, drove me on my knees to the Merciful Isis, that in the silence of the hours of darkness, she might better hear my prayers.

"Every tenth year, those among the people of the white and purple robes who are about to become mothers approach the hour of their travail in mental torture lest the new born be a girl. For every girl babe born to the wise and the legal ones during this year, belongs to the Nation until she has passed her twentieth year. For her must be only the highest standards of mental, moral and physical upbringing. She is taught the language of the owl people from the time she learns to lisp her native tongue. She must also know the fabled speech of the mythical race who are said to live beyond the river of fire.

"Her life is a cloistered, secluded one. Her body is builded to its utmost perfection, her education provided for by Vesuvian law.

"For, during the twentieth year of her life, she is one of those few who are eligible to be chosen as High Priestess of the Owl People! Only the daughters of the counselors or of royal lineage are considered to have the inherent wisdom necessary to absorb the rigorous course prescribed.

"Once every ten years, usually during the Fete of Sanctity, an envoy of the Owl King appears, as did the one today. Out of the eligibles, one is chosen by lottery to be taken into the heart of the vast forest and to rule over the feathered tribe for the next decade. The others, the ones who are not chosen, are freed from the menace forever, as only a virgin in her twentieth year may be so chosen. Twenty years ago, ten girls were born to the prescribed classes. Tomorrow, nine of us face the ordeal; tomorrow, eight go free!"

"And the tenth? She died in childhood, perhaps?"

A convulsive shudder swept through the girl's frame.

"Would that she had! Regardless of the precepts she had been taught, despite the warnings dinned in her ears from early youth---she loved---unwisely! Last year at the Fete of Sanctity she received the punishment reserved for those who break this rigid law. Banishment to the edge of the great forest, on the back of a stalwart Bubon, where she must bathe in the River of Fire! "

"But, Alethea, you say that a new Priestess is chosen every tenth year. What, then, becomes of the others?"

"That is what makes it so frightful---the uncertainty, the lack of knowledge, the whispered legends of the Dark Forest. I almost wish I had died in the arena this afternoon. Better known death than a future fraught with undreamed of horrors. None has ever returned to tell the tale."

"But you say it is a lottery, a drawing. Surely your chance is equal to that of the others."

"It is my one hope---a hope that I cling to with all the power for courage that is left within me. And yet---I am afraid."

She broke off suddenly. When she spoke again it was with forced lightness. Carson admired her for her bravery, her fortitude.

"Come, my friend, let us talk of pleasanter things. Let the morrow take care of itself. Perhaps, after all, it will find me free---to let you prove yourself more than a friend to me!"

Her eyes were shining through unshed tears, shining with a light that glows but once in a woman's eyes; a glow that burns and gleams eternally or, hopes shattered, dies out never to be rekindled!

No one slept that night in the house of Maestro. The early hours of the morning, before the light of day flashed on, were spent in silent prayer before the images of Isis that Alethea set up before an improvised altar. Carson could picture similar scenes being enacted in eight other houses that night and mentally blasphemed the ancestors of this wonder-girl who could be inveigled into making this a part of their treaty with the Bubons, no matter what it would have cost to keep the womanhood of the land immune.

"This time, as they made their way through the

crowded streets to the Forum, Alethea walked at Joe Carson' side. As companions of one of the potential victims, they were allotted a place near the edge of the crude platform which had sprung up overnight and on which some of the girls had already taken their places. Bidding the men good-bye, Alethea joined them.

The throng parted, and down the passageway thus formed came the trio who seemed synchronal with the coming of unjust destiny. In the middle, towering high above the dwarfed ruler, was the feathered messenger of the Owl King. At his right, Romulo, while on the left came the inevitable Bunos in his saffron garb. On his left arm, the priest carried an urn of gold, while in his right hand he bore a yellow bag, whose contents jingled ominously as he ascended the platform. He placed the urn at his side of the platform nearest Carson, and stepped back while Romulo took the center of the stage.

The Emperor's slit of a mouth opened. His voice boomed like the knell of doom.

"Twice before, in my regime, have I presided over a like ceremony. Twice before have I seen one of the daughters of Vesuvia chosen to reign over the people of the great forest for a decade. Once again it is within my province to preside at such an occasion so that our treaty with Bubo and his people may be fulfilled .

"As is the custom, as is the law, Bunos has inscribed upon the discs of gold the names of each girl. These will be placed in the urn, well-shaken, and one selected. It is in the hands of fate and the Gods .

"As also is the custom, and the law, someone from the

multitude must be chosen to make the choice. We have among us a stranger from another land, the white-skinned youth who shattered our tradition only yesterday, and whose valor caused the commoners to plead for his life despite his indiscretions. What more fitting than that, in my clemency and mercy, I honor him by electing him the one to pick the coin."

Whatever else could be said about Romulo, he knew his mob psychology. Cries came from all parts of the vast throng.

"Romulo is just!"

"Romulo is merciful!"

"Romulo is magnanimous in his forgiveness!"

Carson felt himself lifted to the platform. For a fleeting moment he caught the Emperor's eye, caught the malicious gleam that lurked behind his benignant pose. What trickery was this arch schemer up to now? What new devilment was he planning, or what plot had already been laid?

Romulo motioned him to a place beside the girls. Bunos stepped forward, opened the yellow bag, and passed a golden disc to the ruler who called the name of a girl.

One of those on the platform stepped forward. Romulo crossed to the urn and dropped the disc inside. One by one the girls were called, 'till only Alethea remained. She, too, stepped forward, as Romulo intoned her name.

The urn was shaken so that there was no possibility of anyone choosing any particular coin. Then the High Priest placed it in the center of the platform, while the girls formed a half-circle about it. Romulo stepped forward and beckoned

Carson to join him. He pointed at the urn of Fate and spoke but a single word:

"Choose!"

Joe Carson reached his hand into the golden container. His fingers closed over a coin. He did not dare look to see what name was inscribed upon it but, palm still closed, he stretched forth his arm and dropped the fatal disc into Romulo's waiting hand.

CHAPTER XI
WINGS OF DESPAIR

An awed hush swept over the crowd. Romulo paused impressively. Once more he spoke but a single word.

"Alethea!"

The world seemed to sway before Joe Carson's eyes. His hand had been the one to send the girl to her doom. So that was the reason Romulo had selected him to pick the coin! But how could he have known that Alethea's name would be chosen?

Struck by sudden suspicion, Carson's hand swept deep into the urn, came out clutching several of the coins. He scanned them hastily. So that was the solution of Romulo's perfidy.

On every one of the golden discs he held, Alethea's name was inscribed !

But Joe Carson was never to announce his discovery to the assembled throng. Fast as he had moved, Romulo had been faster. Already the platform swarmed with Amazonic guards. Once more Joe Carson was a prisoner. At a signal, Bunos stepped to the front of the platform and silenced the buzz of conversation with raised hand. His dead, monotonous voice droned out his message like a voice from a tomb.

"It is written that, save for the coin selected, no hand save that of the High Priest and of the Emperor shall touch the discs of gold. Such sacrilege even the mercy of Romulo cannot condone. The punishment is also written into the code---banishment to the edge of the great forest, to purge his sins in the River of Fire."

He turned to the owl and spoke in the guttural tongue of the bird, then turned to address the crowd once more.

"At the close of this ceremony, he shall be cast into the dungeon, to await the return of one of the people of Bubo, who shall bear him to his doom."

Then, gathering the golden discs which Carson had scattered about the floor of the platform, he returned them to the golden urn and clapped his hands. Two of the black pygmies appeared upon the platform with cords of woven silver and gold. Then the High Priest led Alethea to where the owl waited.

Murmuring an incantation, he removed her tunic of white. Priest and Emperor lifted her to the back of the monster bird, and held her in place while the slaves bound her fast with the heavy cords.

His heart filled with anguish and abject woe, Joe Carson watched as the bird spread his mammoth wings, and rose slowly above the heads of the throng. Three times it circled the crowd, each time rising higher and higher. Then, turning in the direction of the vast forest of Titanic trees, it sped 'till it was but a black speck against the sky.

But in Joe Carson's ears was the shirring of wings---wings of despair that threatened to eat out his heart, to drive him into frenetic foolhardiness. Prompted by the spears of his Amazonic captors, he permitted himself to be led away, yearning all the while for a chance to meet this deformed demon who ruled Vesuvia face to face---alone. With bare fists, he would beat that hideous face to unrecognizable pulp---then he would be willing to die; with Alethea gone there would be nothing left to live for. Once inside the dark cell of the ancient prison, he gave himself up to gloomy retrospection.

He did not know how long he mused thus, giving himself over to thoughts black as the shades of Niflheim. At last came inspiration.

He was not one of this inner world. Why need he fret about its peoples or its punishments. Even now, upon the earth, six men waited for his return. He had promised to be back within four days. This was the third he had spent in this alien land. Allowing for the difference in time, even now his friends must be waiting anxiously for some word or sign that he was safe and sound. He would wait until the hours of darkness, then he would go back to the land from whence he came and leave this recreation of a long dead land behind.

But what of Alethea? He could not leave her in this manner. She was the magnet which, unconsciously, had drawn him here. She was his, no matter what the laws and customs of Vesuvia might say to the contrary.

Go back to the earth he must and would, but he would return---not to the cell in this dismal dungeon, but to the land of the Bubons. Here he would find the girl who meant more to him than life itself, here he would fight her battles as well as his own.

If only he could get some word to Maestro. The news of his escape must come to the historian's ears, and he would draw but one conclusion, that he had taken the easiest way when danger threatened, and returned to his own land and safety. But how could he let him know?

A stealthy tread outside his cell door, a whispered voice---the voice of Ornoco!

"Speak quietly, or I may be discovered. One of the guards let me slip through awhile, for pay."

Swiftly, clearly, Carson outlined his plan.

"By mid-day tomorrow, if all goes well, I should be in the land of the Bubons," he concluded. "Unless ill befalls me, each night, at the fifth hour of darkness, my astral self will come to your home and let you know what is going on. Perhaps you can devise some plan to help me."

Ornoco groped through the darkness, found his hand, and wrung it warmly.

"Go, my friend, and may Isis walk beside you! I shall tell my father, and he will add his prayers to my own for your safe return."

CHAPTER XII
THE WANDERER RETURNS

In the room in Professor Greyland's home, six staid spectacled scientists sat in somber silence watching the last few hours of the fourth day tick away.

It was almost midnight when their senses quickened, and with one accord they strove to draw the physical self of Joe Carson back across the immeasurable gulf of the infinite by the sheer power of their mighty wills.

They felt the nearness of his astral self as he fused his mental strength with their own. One last, mighty effort---and Joe Carson stood before them, gripping Professor Greyland's hand!

He dressed hastily as the scientists grouped around him, plying him with questions. Gone was the whimsical smile, in its place a look of grim determination.

"Gentlemen, with your help I have carried through. I have much to tell you. Things that, as scientists, you may be loathe to believe. But, as surely as I have succeeded in proving the practicability of my theory, just so surely is that which I have to tell you, true!

"I am tired. The trip has been an arduous one. Food, drink, a little sleep, and I will tell you all."

At dawn, after a few hours of fitful slumber, he faced the semi-circle once more. At his request, Professor Greyland took down his story as he unfolded it before an audience of six keen, analytical, unbiased, scientific minds. And as he talked, the eyes of the learned ones widened, filled with awe at his revelations. In absolute silence save for the turning of the pages in the Professor's note-book, Joe Carson told his tale .

"And now," he concluded, "God willing, I shall return. I feel that I must carry on the task I have assigned myself. Once more, gentlemen, I am going to ask your cooperation.

"This time it should prove easier. Our minds are in perfect accord. All of us know my destination. I do not know how long it will take to complete the task, but I will try to report to you within the next two weeks, little more than ten days in Vesuvian time. Today is the twenty-second of February---say not later than the seventh of March."

The scientists tried to dissuade him, but Carson was obdurate.

"I have given my word. I must keep it if it is humanly possible for me to do so. If you will not assist me, I must attempt the transmutation alone, but I feel that without your added mental strength I am foredoomed to failure.

"Time is pressing. Already it is nearly nine. I must have your answer, now."

A brief discussion and the occultists acquiesced. Once more the scientists formed a circle about the cot; once more Joe Carson stretched at full length upon it and closed his eyes. Again, six minds concentrated to speed him on his way.

A few minutes after nine, for the second time Professor Greyland reverently gathered up a heap of empty clothes and draped them across the back of a chair.

The Vengeful Vision

BEHIND THE CLOSED DOOR of his private office, Caleb Morrissy rubbed his burning ears. He needed neither dictaphone nor power of telepathy to determine the cause of the burning. He knew exactly what was being thought and whispered by the handful of clerks in the outer room. It was the same every year. Because he did not pass out goldpieces, turkeys or meaningless Yuletide cheer, these hare-brained salary-snatchers catalogued him as a 20th century Scrooge! Damn Christmas . . . and all the bitter associations it brought to his mind!

He chewed savagely at his unlighted cigar and watched the racing clock hands. Eleven already! Five short hours to train time! Each year he solemnly swore that this would be his last to make the pilgrimage! Each year, he broke his vow. He knew that four o'clock would find him on the train, and once more his holiday would be spent in surroundings which would grate on his nerves like the rasping of a gigantic file.

At precisely 3:30, snugly wrapped in his fur-lined great-coat, his hat pulled down over his eyes, he strode in sullen silence through the outer office and slammed the door behind him without so much as a parting glance at his employees, heads bent low over their desks in well-simulated activity.

In the street, he brusquely elbowed his way through the festive throng; men whose arms were loaded with bundles of assorted shapes and sizes; women with eager children tugging at their skirts or stopping stock still to gaze at some new wonder; grotesque Santa Clauses standing guard over open kettles that by the morrow would contain enough money to provide dinners and cheer for the worthy poor . . . an eager, happy crowd that refused to be disturbed by his muttered snarls. He shut his eyes to the evidences of holiday spirit which flanked him on every side . . . the gaily festooned shop-windows . . . the holly wreaths, crystallized grasses and helichrysms that lusty-voiced vendors urged on the passing celebrators . . . the municipal tree that glowed in the mall before the Union Station. It was only a short walk from office to depot, yet, despite his dogged haste, it was two minutes before the hour when he finally wedged himself into a seat in the crowded train.

Ensconced behind a newspaper, using his cigar to provide a smoke-screen that would shelter him from the eyes of the jovial excursionist, he settled back to passive endurance of the distasteful ride. An hour later, he stood on the station platform at Bayboro, peering through the murky dusk for the vehicle which was to take him to his destination.

A dilapidated carryall drawn by a decrepit nag! An

archaism in this age of horseless carriages and winged motors! Another condescension to that first observance of a quarter-century ago. He shuddered slightly. Yes, there it was, looming up through the gathering shadows like a spectre of the past. An old Negro, rheumatic and bent, hobbled up to where he waited.

"Yessuh! Lemme take yo' grip, suh! Ah's been waitin' hyah fo' dat dyar train 'till Ah tho't Ah'd freeze stiffer'n starch! Clim' right en an' Ah'll tuck yo' up so's yo'll be comf'ble. 'Right, suh?' 'Dep, Betsy!"

Another stretch of torturous travel ahead! In a few moments they left the lights of the little city behind. If the deliberate progress of the local had irked him, this leisurely jogging over abominable rutted roads tormented him to the point of downright wretchedness.

He looked about him at the desolate landscape. He knew every turn of the long road, the location of each farmhouse that stood silhouetted against the overcast sky, the snow-covered meadows which reached to the very edge of the wooded swampland which, in its turn, stretched most of the fifty miles from Bayboro to Fenham; land that never had been reclaimed because of its tenacious quagmires and sucking quicksands.

Christmas Eve! The surroundings emphasized the blasphemous mockery of the phrase! He laughed---a harsh, strange laugh that made the Negro glance askance over his shoulder and urge Betsy into a half-hearted trot.

At last horse, driver and passenger turned into a driveway arched with the interlocked arms of centuried elms. Caleb Morrissy gave a sigh of relief---then caught his breath at a suddenly remembered fear.

The house that stood at the end of the canopied lane was stern and foreboding. From gabled eaves to cloistered cellar it was a fit abode for maleficent forces. Heavy black curtains, tightly drawn behind diamond-paned windows, penned all light within. A heartless, sinister, nefarious house that conjured visions of legendary days when witchcraft and necromancy held sway.

Caleb alighted and mounted the steps while the Negro limped away into the night with the tired horse. Without knocking, he lifted the latch and pushed his way into a dimly lighted hall.

A man with bowed head waited for him in the semi-darkness. He vouch-safed his guest a brief nod of greeting as the latter doffed his wraps and hung them on the antique hat-tree.

"You're late, Caleb."

"The train, Iric---as usual." He waved a hand in the direction of the stable. "Noah will tell you." He followed his host along the hall and into the dining-room.

The long table was laid for three. Iric Stoughton took his place at the head and motioned the other to the seat at his left. Caleb Morrissy slipped into it with averted gaze. The unoccupied chair at the foot of the table did not particularly disturb him, though it helped stimulate his disconcerting memories---that had been vacant, now, for thirty years; since Ella Stoughton's soul had passed on, the night her daughter was born. It was the other he feared to face---the one directly opposite him, where the third place was laid. He knew exactly what he would find before he steeled himself to the inevitable and raised his eyes!

Not merely another empty chair, but a monument to shattered hopes and dreams! A chair draped from high back to floor in a solemn, sable shroud! For a generation he had occupied this same seat on Christmas Eve, had eaten his holiday fare with the same dismal memorial to depress him. Already Chloe was bustling about the table with steaming dishes---dishes of purest white, each rimmed with a wide, black, mourning band!

Supper was a perfunctory affair. Caleb stole an occasional glance at the face of his host---wan, drawn, lined with poignant grief and deep-felt pain. At such brief espials, Caleb's eyes would glow with a momentary flash of impious gratification and the corners of his mouth turn upward in the vague suggestion of a smile. But eyes and lips reverted to their former melancholy as he would face the cenotaph across the table once more. The men ate but little and Chloe's ebony face was lined with concern as they pushed back their chairs and prepared to rise. She watched them as they crossed the room and vanished through the heavy folds of the jet portieres. It was an old story to her, this Yuletide ceremonial, yet, despite its familiarity, she brushed away a tear as she turned to her task of clearing away the half-emptied dishes, at the thought of two grown men inexorably committed to such penitent parody on the spirit of the day---well though she knew the tragedy which prompted their behaviour !

In the far corner of the room in which the men now found themselves, in the shadows between one of the black-shaded windows and the old-fashioned fireplace, was the first evidence that this, after all, was Christmas Eve---a stately evergreen, whose topmost boughs grazed the high ceiling, while at its base was banked a wealth of toys.

But both men knew the irony in that first erroneous impression; both knew exactly what stark reality would stand revealed in the shifting lights that played upon the scene from the long fire. In these eerie, dancing lights the tree seemed to jeer at them, its branches became mocking fingers---a tree trimmed with darksome garlands of silken crape!

Among the motley array of toys a doll held the place of honor---the same doll that on the calamitous night long past had lent chief promise of a happy Christmas morn. A doll whose cheeks had been red with the blush of the rose, and whose gay frock had been a tribute to the art of its designer. The ravages of years had left their traces on this plaything as surely as on the faces of the men who were drawing chairs closer to the open grate and turning them to face the tragic scene. Now, the doll's face was ashen and the vivid dress had been replaced with garb of raven hue. It seemed to mourn for the little mistress who had never clasped it in her arms!

The men lighted cigars and sat in moody silence, eyeing first one another and then the sinister tree and its taunting treasures. All night long they would sit with their torturous thought . . . waiting . . . watching . . . hoping . . . fearing . . .

For the first time since his curt greeting in the hall, Iric Stoughton spoke. The same, brief question he had asked every year for a quarter of a century:

"Do you remember, Caleb?"

"Everything." The same, stereotyped answer, as if the dialogue was some mystic ritual. For the second time that day, Caleb Morrissy turned his cigar into a smoke-screen; this time, to protect himself from the boring, suffering eyes of his host. Remember? Could he ever forget! The gloomy setting before his eyes blacked out, and on the silver-sheet of his memory scenes of bygone days passed in cinematic review.

Fifty years ago, Zachariah Morrissy had moved from Fenham to Bayboro with his wife and only child, a lad of five. He brought with him his hoarded dollars; dollars grown from pennies eked out by years of hard labor on his Fenham farm. Five years later, these Morrissy dollars, wisely invested, had won him a substantial place in the community; ten, and he had become a rural nabob. It was the Morrissy mills that had put Bayboro on the mercantile map; that had attracted outside capital and competition; that were directly responsible for the rapid growth of stagnant town to thriving city in less than half a century. He had reached the height of his prosperity while his son was in his teens; the formative age, the time when a youth's character is moulded by the influences that surround him. A doting mother, with a false conception of wealth and power, fostered by sudden affluence after years of penury, had pampered the boy, indulged his every whim, 'till by the time Caleb attained his majority the idea was firmly fixed in his mind that it was the world's duty to feed him caviar from a diamond-studded spoon.

A life of luxurious idleness just suited Caleb. He admired his father's business acumen and Yankee courage, but he admired far more the early morning canters into the nearby woods, the long afternoons of indolent ease and the evenings of dissolute recreation with others of his social sphere. He openly resented his father's insistent demands that he perpetuate the name of Morrissy in the business world, but when it came to a clash of wills, his was no match for the older man's adamant one. He refused, point-blank, however, to go into the Morrissy mills and learn the business from the ground up, and his mother backed him loyally in his stand. At last it was settled that Caleb should find a niche in the mart of commerce, of his own or his mother's choosing. That suited Caleb! Either way, he was sure of as easy a berth as money could buy.

The firm of Stoughton and Son was the most reputable brokerage house in Bayboro. For years the elder Stoughton had handled investments for the cautious merchants of the city, and had impressed them with his consistently sound advice and Puritanical integrity. Even Zachariah was pleased when his son established a connection with this staid and well-esteemed concern.

It was there that Caleb's acquaintance with Iric Stoughton began. It was through Iric that he met Ella Mather. From the very first, Caleb desired her---a desire that was intensified when for the first time in his life he found himself unable to procure immediately that which he desired. He could hardly be blamed for his passion; scarcely an eligible male in their circle did not view her with covetous eyes. She was a bewitching, fragile flower---a lily from the Divine Garden.

Caleb was no fool. He was quick to sense the fact that the girl favored Iric Stoughton. He made it a point to cultivate the young broker that he might come into more frequent contact with her. Slowly, yet surely, he knew that she was yielding to his persuasive tongue and persistent love-making.

Then, just as he was positive he had won, warned perhaps by the proverbial intuition of her sex that his ardor was prompted by jealous desire rather than sacred love, Ella Mather announced her engagement to Iric Stoughton.

Caleb wrung his rival's hand warmly in congratulation, while in his heart sprouted noxious weeds of lasting hate. Idle tongues found cause for wagging in his cheerful fortitude. They gossiped still more when he was best man at the wedding. But while he smiled and wished them happiness, his treacherous mind cast about for some means of retaliation. With an elephant's singleness of purpose his brain harbored dire thoughts of ultimate revenge. He must bide his time, plan carefully; then strike suddenly and effectively.

It was shortly afterward, he had just passed his twenty-third birthday, when the elder Stoughton died. Here was his opportunity to lay a firmer foundation for the satiation of his inveterate enmity. Iric Stoughton had no inkling of his secret resolutions,---he accepted Caleb at face value as true friend and boon companion. The firm name was altered to *Stoughton and Morrissy.*

Two years more swept by. Just as the first of his schemes of retaliation neared maturity, Fate stepped into the game. A child was born in the Stoughton home, and the soul of a broken lily was transplanted in the Garden of Eternity.

Caleb was the first to offer carefully phrased condolences; but all the while his heart chortled in impious glee. He felt no particular pangs over the death of Ella Stoughton, she had been irretrievably lost to him the night she had become a bride; but he took an unholy pleasure in watching the bereaved man as he resumed his daily duties. It was as if he was spying on a soul bared for the world to see its suffering. He knew the depth of the love Iric Stoughton had borne his mate; knew, too, the depth of sorrow Iric Stoughton would bear.

His joy was short-lived. The child was a miniature of her mother; the same gossamer beauty, the same ephemeral fragility. Iric Stoughton found relief from his bitterness in a new devotion---a worship that even Caleb could never fully understand.

At the insistence of his partner, Caleb became a frequent visitor at the Stoughton home. The cameo-likeness of the baby to her mother grew more marked day by day. Every sight of the child renewed his jealous hate, his baffled feeling that, even in Death, Ella Stoughton had thwarted him.

A year passed . . . three . . . five. Evening after evening he had held the tiny tot upon his knee or heard her baby lips lisp goodnight prayers. She called him "Uncle" Caleb and made a place for him in her lovable heart second only to her beloved dad. But while her eyes widened at the stories he told of elves and gnomes and witches, his mind was busy with the cankerous thought that somehow---sometime---this innocent lass might prove the medium of his long deferred revenge.

Then came the memorable Christmas Eve of a quarter-century ago. Windows hung with cheery wreaths of holly and poinsettias, each brightened with three gleaming candles . . . happy childish laughter . . . excited prattle of Santa Claus and sleigh bells . . . slender baby fingers hanging sparkling strands of tinsel to high branches of the mammoth tree, from the vantage point of "Uncle" Caleb's shoulders . . .

cornucopias . . . strings of popcorn . . . stockings hung by the fireplace . . friendly flames from the blazing logs . . . hustle . . . hustle . . . confusion . . .

Ready for bed at last, her tiny white hand smothered in Chloe's rough black one, supremely happy from head to little bare toes, the dainty maid paused in the arched doorway and threw farewell kisses to her dad and her "Uncle" Caleb. The dancing lights from the open grate transformed her golden ringlets into a shining halo and turned her sparkling eyes into blue pools of laughing water. The spotless nightgown lent an ethereal touch . . . she became an airy sprite . . . a seraphic fay . . . a diminutive Spirit of Christmas!

Iric Stoughton sped across the room and folded his daughter in his hungry arms. Kiss after kiss he rained upon her soft cheeks, the nape of her neck, her bare pink toes.

"I'll go up with her tonight, Chloe---it's Christmas Eve! No, never mind the lamp, I know the old hall like a book. Here---this will do." He caught up a lighted candle from the nearby window sill and the pair headed across the dining-room to the stairway which led up into the west wing of the dwelling. A short time later Caleb heard the door at the foot of the stairs click softly and Iric reappeared among them. Subconsciously, Caleb noticed that the candle had been left upstairs .

Then came busy moments that passed all too swiftly, moments when hidden bundles were retrieved from drawers, chests and cupboards, the tree loaded with goodies, the stockings filled, the base of the tree banked with trinkets and toys to gladden the heart of the sleeping child on Christmas morn, the clutter of papers and twine cleared away. If Caleb stayed away longer than was absolutely necessary on one of his trips away from the cheery parlor, he purchased full forgiveness for his absence with the doll he unwrapped on his return---the doll that was given the place of honor, the toy that would be first to catch her eager eyes---"Uncle" Caleb's gift to the idol of his partner's heart! At last the laborers stood off to survey the result of their handiwork.

Noah had noticed it, first, as he carried an armful of paper to the kitchen---a faint trace, so vague that he dismissed it as mere imagination---old paper sometimes smelled that way. As the quartet inspected their work, his nostrils quivered and he turned to his wife, a trace of fear in his eyes:

"Listen hyar, Chloe, duz yo' smell smoke, or am Ah dreamin'?"

Iric Stoughton caught the hoarse whisper, the quaver in his tone.

"Nonsense, Noah!" he interpolated, "Where?"

"Ah doan like to think so, suh, but 'pears to me as how it's from upstahs."

Upstairs! Iric's face blanched at the hinted horror. The nursery! His child! With a bound he sprang for the other room, Caleb close on his heels. There was no doubt of it. Here the acrid odor was clearly defined and a vagrant wisp curled through the jamb of the closed door at the foot of the stairway. With trembling hand, he turned the knob and flung it wide!

Heavy clouds of thick smoke enveloped him; smoke that filled his lungs and eyes as he hurdled the stairs three at a time. Savage tongues of flame licked the woodwork at the far end of the hall. He was dimly conscious that Caleb and

Noah were close behind him as he fought his way through the stifling air to the door of the nursery---only to balked by a seething mass of fiery destruction. It took the combined efforts of the two men at his side to check his mad dash for the heart of this inferno. He struggled in their grasp with insane fury until, overcome by the horror that lay behind that wall of flame, he collapsed in Noah's arms.

Meanwhile, Chloe had raced out into the night to summon aid. Soon the house was filled with stalwart men and husky boys from adjacent farmhouses. It was Caleb who led the fight against the ravenous menace as pail after pail of water was passed by willing hands up the smoke-filled stairway and down the long hall-but the hungry flames only hissed their vituperation as they turned the water into steam. Their heroic efforts kept the fire from spreading, but by the time the Bayboro fire department arrived the west wing was a charred mass of wreck and ruin. By dawn the sooty, sorrowing neighbors wended their way homeward to carry to waiting wives and mothers grim tidings of the Christmas tragedy.

For weeks the stricken man hovered on the borderline of the Beyond, but medical science triumphed. It was a changed Iric Stoughton who took up his daily tasks once more; grim-visaged, taciturn, his hair prematurely streaked with gray. At times he would sit for hours at his desk and stare with unseeing eyes at the office walls; at others, he would attack his work with vicious intensity as if by ceaseless labor he could close his mind to the grief gnawing at his soul.

But Caleb Morrissy was not satisfied. His rancor had become an obsession. To him, Iric's woe was but an infinitesimal portion of the burden he must bear as the years rolled on. It was Caleb who reminded Iric that he had left the lighted candle in the bedroom. Somehow---someway---this must have been the cause of the fire. There was no other logical explanation. Perhaps the child had wakened and decided to come downstairs . . . she had brushed the candle against her filmy nightgown. Then, too, he pointed out, Iric had closed the door at the foot of the stairs. The nursery had been at the far end of the west wing. With the excitement attendant on the trimming of the tree, with that door closed to keep the sounds from disturbing the sleeping child, it would work as well the other way---no sounds of her pitiful screams would reach them, no telltale smoke warn them until it was too late. He hammered these theories at Iric with systematic ferocity until the agonized mind of the man accepted them as fact---that he had killed his own child as surely by his carelessness as though he had slain her with his two, bare hands!

It was Caleb, as the anniversary of the tragedy grew near, who suggested the dismal ceremonial which had persisted for a generation. It was Caleb's warped mind that had conceived each gruesome detail, the tree trimmed in crape, the dishes with their rims of mourning, the sable-shrouded chair, the doll with its dismal dress of solemn hue. To Iric, it became an annual shrine of penitence; to Caleb it was a promise that the memory of that other night would never cease to plague and torment the crushed and broken man he hated.

As the weeks passed, Iric leaned more and more upon his partner. Soon the bulk of the firm's business passed through Caleb's hands. Morrissy could scarcely keep his joy from showing in his eyes. In November, three years later, Caleb shook the dust of Bayboro from his feet and launched out for himself in a more metropolitan sphere---his capital the money that had once been Iric Stoughton's . He left behind him the hollow shell of a man who gripped his hand at parting and shed honest tears at the loss of his partner and his closest friend---left him to start once more at the foot of the ladder with hypocritical words of cheer and admonition.

Iric's last words had been of the approaching holidays and he had exacted Caleb's promise to join him in the Yuletide ceremonial. To himself, Caleb vowed he would never return, but Christmas Eve found him in his accustomed place before the taunting tree---just as he had been there every Christmas Eve since---just as he was here, tonight!

Penitence? Conscience? Remorse at some unguessed part he had played in the tragedy which had made possible his maniacal vengeance? Whatever the motive, the result was the same! Each year he had faced the pilgrimage with growing disquietude; tonight, he felt that something was about to snap in his harassed brain. The intolerable stillness! If Iric would only speak once in a while instead of sitting there like some vague accusing entity! He tossed the stub of his cigar into the open grate and lighted another. He glanced at the clock on the mantel. Not yet midnight---and it would be dawn before Iric Stoughton would relax his contrite vigil! He wondered if he could endure the long hours ahead. Of one thing he was certain, this was the last time he would attend this sinister satire of his own creating! He had said that many times before, but this time---somehow---he was *Sure*! He stole another glance at the clock. It must have stopped! He stared for a full minute at the lagging hands and listened for its faint ticking. No, it was still going.

The flickering firelight wove everchanging phantasies on the walls, the tree, the funeral shades; grotesque images that bobbed and danced like skeletal marionettes. They personified, magnificently, the chaotic thoughts which raced through Caleb Morrissy's brain. He followed their weird gyrations as they shifted eerily about the room; here ... there . . . everywhere. He thought it odd that the sable portieres should catch and hold the reflection of the fire so long---even after the sportive shadows had leaped to distant points. Each time they touched the spot the light grew stronger, 'till Caleb found himself staring at the curtained archway with unfeigned intentness. He brushed a trembling hand before his eyes. Was it but a reflection of the restless flames? The steel of his fear yielded to the magnet of his curiosity and once more his eyes focused on the glowing spot.

A shining halo that became a wealth of golden curls . . . blue eyes that sparkled like pools of laughing water . . . tiny bare feet peeking shyly from beneath a robe of spotless white . . . baby fingers tossing goodnight kisses . . . a diminutive Spirit of Christmas! A face framed in yellow serpents that were coiled to strike . . . eyes that glinted with the cold blue steel . . . relentless feet that pursued him from unearthly realms . . . charred feet protruding from a flame-flecked shroud . . . slender fingers pointing in stern accusation . . . an atomic Até!

A mad cry cut the sepulchral silence of the room---a shriek that roused Iric Stoughton from his lethargy and brought Noah and Chloe to his side. The trio shrank in wild-eyed horror from the man who rocked to and fro upon his knees before the jet draperies and listened as he mouthed insane petitions to an invisible presence.

"Iric left the candle . . . he is the one to blame . . . why didn't you waken? . . . scream? . . . you were another Ella . . . the bedding caught like tinder . . . you'll forget when you see the doll . . . a glorious doll . . . you're dead, I say! . . . Iric . . . the candle . . . the doll . . . the doll! . . . ."

The silent watchers drew closer to the wall as the gibbering maniac half-crawled across the room and snatched the doll from its place at the foot of the crape-trimmed tree. They shuddered anew as he crooned to it, cradled it in his arms. They watched in hypnotic apathy as he rose, still clasping the time-worn toy, and swayed drunkenly back to the heavy portieres---and through them!

It was not until the outside door slammed behind the fugitive that the spell was broken. With one accord, the trio sprang in pursuit. Through dining room and dimly-lighted hall they sped; out the door and down the canopied lane to the roadway. There, Iric Stoughton halted them and pointed to where Caleb Morrissy, hunched low over the black-frocked doll, fled across the snow meadows and vanished in the tangled maze of wooded swampland in the background .

Realization came slowly to Iric Stoughton. Bit by bit he correlated the maniacal babblings with that horrible night of twenty-five years ago. He had never dreamed of Caleb's hostility---his jealous vindictiveness. Why, Caleb had been his partner, his dearest friend! Vaguely he recalled from the depths of his subconsciousness that Caleb had been gone from the parlor much longer than was necessary when he left to get the doll. Mentally he pictured what must have happened: a skulking figure stealing stealthily up the stairs and into the nursery . . . eyes of hate looking down upon childish innocence and love . . . the candle upon the dresser and the hideous suggestion it had brought to the warped mind of the man he trusted . . . sheets bursting into sudden flame . . . quick, silent flight back to the festivities below, closing all doors behind . . . the hypocritical unwrapping of the doll---the doll he knew would never feel its little mistress' arms!

Iric reviewed the days that had followed. It was Caleb who had convinced him that he was the guilty man; Caleb who had devised the devilish details of this annual mockery; Caleb, he saw now, whose craft had been responsible for his financial failure.

But Iric Stoughton felt no bitterness in his heart against this man who had reared a monster of Hate that, like the Frankenstein creation it was, had turned upon and destroyed him. That feeling of bitterness might come later, but now his eyes shone with a magic light of new-found happiness and a carol of contentment surged through him at the thought that his years of penitence were over. This was his Christmas gift---the knowledge that his soul was free from guilt, that he need grieve no more!

Head up, shoulders back, a renewed lightness in his tread, he helped the servants remove the mocking crape from the stately tree and toss it in the flickering fire. With his own hands he ripped the black covering from the empty chair, and raised the dismal shades as the first streak of dawn tinged the sky. He peered down the shaded driveway as though his eyes could penetrate the depths of the wooded swampland where the madman had fled . . . heedless of its grasping, slimy tentacles . . . chanting delirious lullabies to a witless doll!

For the first Christmas in a quarter century, Iric Stoughton smiled. The trite words which came slowly from his lips, long unaccustomed to their use, seemed fraught with new and deeper meaning as he extended his hand to Chloe and Noah, in turn:

"A MERRY CHRISTMAS! *A very VERY Merry Christmas!*"

Miscreant From Murania

THE DESK CLERK at the Mansion House was a stranger to me. As I scrawled my signature on the register I could see the name of Dexter meant nothing to him. After all, time brings changes even in a town like Trestle.

He chose a key from the rack, came out from behind the desk, picked up my suitcases and guided me up the worn staircase to my room on the floor above. He dropped my grips by the foot of the old wooden double bed, opened the window, put the key in the lock, and grunted at the quarter I dropped into his open palm and closed the door quietly behind him.

I was already calling myself a darn fool for yielding to the impulse that had prompted me to drive eleven hundred miles just to spend a few hours in my home town. It must have been the show-off in me. I'd day dreamed all the way home about the furore it would create when I drove into town in my brand new, high-powered shiny black roadster, my pockets bulging with bills, and sporting the best in tailor-made clothes.

So what happened? So far, absolutely nothing. I'd hit town about half an hour ago, practically inched the car along the whole length of Main Street and back again, and not one person had given me a tumble.

I wasn't too much surprised to find the business center with its face lifted. The upstairs movie house had been converted into offices and a new theater replaced Pop Dodson's general store. I noted a chain market and a new post office. Even Joe's Tonsorial Parlor sported a neon-lighted barber pole. But, somehow, I got the impression that behind this big-town front I'd find the people still had the same, small-town minds.

As far as I could see, the Mansion House was still the only hotel. So here I was, my car parked in the big open area between the street and the hotel, in front of the long porch that ran the entire length of the wide fronted structure.

The long drive had been hot and enervating. One look in the mirror at the dark stubble discoloring my chin and I knew exactly what I needed, the kind of relaxation a man finds only in a barber's chair. I wondered if Joe Parker would remember his one-time Saturday shoe shine boy. This time I walked the short distance from the hotel.

I recognized him the moment I stepped inside the door. The same, round, full face, the same bald spot on top of his head, the same jovial smile and chatterbox manner. The only evidence of the passing years was a trace of gray just above his temples. But, even here, there had been changes. The back room, where the regulars used to hold their bull sessions, was gone. The rear third of the shop was cut off by a wall board partition with an entrance at one end. Above the opening was the legend, "Manicurist." Joe had a customer, and half a dozen men lounged in chairs arranged against the wall.

It looked like I was due for a longer wait than I'd anticipated. I dropped into a vacant seat, picked up a dog-eared picture magazine and glanced through it aimlessly, both ears open for any stray bits of gossip about the town.

I didn't even have time to get comfortably settled. Joe finished combing his customer's hair, whisked away the protective covering with a flourish, and called "Next," with a look in my direction. I gave an inquisitive nod towards the men who were ahead of me. Joe shook his head.

"You're next, mister. They're waiting for manicures."

I chuckled as I slid into the barber's chair. I'd grown up in Trestle, and the idea of six men in Joe's place waiting for a manicure struck me funny.

"Haircut and a shave."

Something in my voice must have rung a bell in Joe's mind. He swung the swivel chair so that the light would show my face more clearly. He seized my chin, looked deep into my eyes.

"Either I'm nuts or you're Pete Dexter!"

"Right on the button, Hawkeye! You're wasting time on this job. If you were the sheriff, no known criminal would dare to hit this burg. By the way, how's crime these days?"

That last crack was a flashback to old times, a running gag with which we used to greet one another. Trestle was a crimeless town. The only workout the jail ever got was as a temporary lodging for some of the boys who hit the bottle a little too hard. After all, we had to collect enough fines to pay the sheriff's salary. Joe's reaction was the last thing I expected. His eyes took on a furtive expression. His voice lowered to a whisper.

"The whole town's panicky, Pete. Everybody's scared stiff."

"I'm a stranger in town, remember?"

Joe leaned closer. "Thought maybe that's why you came. Ain't you a private dick?"

"Not when I'm on vacation. What's up, Joe?"

He barely breathed the word into my ear. "Vampires!"

All I could think of was a man with long teeth. I couldn't hold back the laughter. Joe shook my shoulders hard.

"Cut it. "Taint funny. Chickens and rabbits have been missing from the farms for miles around, and the bodies of the ones they found didn't have a drop of blood left in 'em."

"Poppycock! Weasels, most likely, or maybe a fox."

"Not a chance. No tracks. The farmers say the teeth marks were never made by an animal. But that ain't the worst. Four days ago, Tom Webster's kid disappeared, and nobody can find hide nor hair of him!"

The full impact of Joe's news was lost, because at the exact moment I caught sight of the mistress of the files and the curved blades. I've seen many a luscious dish in my travels, but this dame would play second fiddle to none of them. Full, red lips, a form that could have been sculptured by a Pheidias, a sweater and skirt that fit as though she'd been poured into them. I nudged Joe.

"Who is she? Where'd you find her?"

"Name's Myrna. She and her grandfather moved here about four months ago. Took the old Dodson place at the edge of Salem Woods."

"That dump! That old shack was falling apart when I went away!"

"Still is. But the rent's cheap. The old man's bedridden. Myrna has to support both of 'em. She came in here right after they moved in and sold me the idea of giving her a job. My trade's more than doubled!"

"No wonder. Think I could do with a nail job myself."

The gal withdrew into her cubicle with her next client, and I settled back to enjoy Joe's ministrations. My body relaxed under his skillful touch, but my thoughts raced ahead like greyhounds.

So Tom Webster's kid was missing. I knew Tom. His dad was the town banker. Tom had just started in the bank to follow in his father's footsteps about the time I'd left as Trestle's number one draftee. I wondered if he was as much of a snob as he used to be, and who he'd found to marry him. I also wondered how old his youngster was. Kids used to do that often, either in Salem Woods or at the other end of the town around Devil's Swamp, but they always turned up okay after a day or two.

This might be different. Seeing it was George Webster's grandson it could even be kidnapping. A couple of smart operators might be able to cut in for a nice slice of the old coot's bankroll. Why didn't somebody call in the state cops? Or maybe the F.B.I.?

But to blame it on vampires! Silly, superstitious fools. That kind of tommyrot went out with the dawn of the twentieth century. If somebody didn't knock some sense into their heads there was no telling what these country bumpkins might do. History was full of witchcraft burnings in similar New England towns. Only this time it would be a silver bullet or a white-thorn stake driven through the heart.

All this time Joe Parker had been keeping up a running fire of conversation, but I hadn't sensed a word. I suppose he was bringing me up to date on a lot of things I wanted to know about the town. I tuned in on him again.

"You're not going to eat in any restaurant the first night in town after all these years. You're coming out to our place. Wait 'til I call Mame."

He came back from the 'phone as happy as a kid with a new pup.

"Mame says she'll break every bone in your body if you say "No' . . . Won't be no fancy eats, though. Just corned beef and cabbage."

That sold me! I hadn't tasted a real old-fashioned home cooked New England boiled dinner since I'd left Trestle. Joe promised to pick me up at the hotel right after the shop closed.

I was lounging in one of the comfortable chairs on the spacious veranda when his coupe pulled up across the road. Joe lived about four miles from the center, a little off the main highway, about halfway between the Mansion House and Devil's Swamp. He talked about his son Jeff, his two grandchildren, and how lonesome Mame had been since Jeff moved his family to Gladstone.

The moon was bright, the night clear and mild.

Joe and I sat out on the front stoop, pipes alight, at peace with the world. Mame joined us as soon as the dishes were done and the kitchen spick and span. Through a clearing we could see a slice of the state road and the autos whizzing by at express train speed. I was happier than I'd been in a decade.

I saw the weather-beaten car when it cut out of line, watched it creep up on the three machines immediately ahead with a rapidity that suggested it must be a souped-up job. As it swerved suddenly back into its own lane I saw an object drop into the roadway. We heard the strident shriek of brakes as the car following skidded to a sudden stop, the metallic crash as the next automobile failed to halt in time, and the hysterical scream of a terrified woman.

Joe and I headed for the highway as Mame was going towards the 'phone.

Cars were stopping all along the road, their inquisitive occupants hurrying to the scene. One driver was playing traffic cop and directing those with less curiosity through the resultant jam.

We elbowed our way close to the car, and I caught a glimpse of the tiny form crushed beneath the wheel. With a prescience that had served me in good stead in many of my off-trail experiences, I knew before Joe's horror-filled voice confirmed it that it was little Bobby Webster. I knew, too, that his death had not been caused by the guilt-racked driver, that when the authorities arrived they would find the body of the child as completely drained of blood as any of the neighboring farmers' chickens !

By morning, all New England was reading about it---with pictures! I scanned the morning tabloid which had come in from Boston while waiting for breakfast in the hotel dining room. For some reason I felt listless, lethargic. I must be get-ing old if last night's excitement tired me out this much. Another thing, breakfast with me was usually a matter of toast or crullers and coffee, but this morning I'd ordered a full portion of ham and eggs. Maybe a good meal would act as an eye-opener.

A spot on the back of my neck irritated me. I ran my finger under my collar and rubbed it. Joe must have nicked me when he shaved my neck.

But I wanted to read the news, not concentrate on my own feelings. I turned to the paper once more. The supernatural angle was too good to miss, and the vampire theme ran through the story. The paper carried a cartoon of a bug-eyed monster, and infant gripped tightly in its horrible fangs, reaching out hairy hands with long sharp nails toward a group of fleeing tots. Another warned all New Englanders to be on the lookout for a man or woman with a strong, aquiline face, arched nostrils, cruel mouth, sharp white teeth, course broad hands that were cold to the touch, and fine-pointed fingernails. To me it read like something the reporter had cribbed directly from "Dracula."

Trestle, which only yesterday was a pin-point on the map, a whistle-stop, suddenly became a mecca for the morbidly curious, the souvenir hunters, amateur sleuths, news hounds, and others out for a grizzly holiday. They overran the town and the surrounding territory. They combed the area for clues and found nothing. They viewed the scene of the tragedy, snapped pictures, quizzed the inhabitants until they became weary and tight-lipped.

By two in the afternoon the Mansion House, which had only a few guests when I arrived, was filled to over-lowing. The desk clerk seemed completely indifferent to the excitement. He barely looked up as he registered guests, gave out room keys and let the guests find their own way through the hotel.

I drifted about, renewing acquaintances, contacting old friends, and getting the lowdown on things that were going on. The funeral was scheduled for Sunday afternoon. The town council, at a special noon meeting, posted a reward of one thousand dollars. George Webster matched it with a similar sum. He posed for countless photographs, interviewed police and private investigators, issued statements, and adroitly took the spotlight off his son and his daughter-in-law.

With the surging throng of outlanders, the natives were too busy all day for much of anything else. In the late afternoon a bunch of school boys pelted Lem Settle, the town simpleton, with stones, chasing him all the way to the jail---where Sheriff Briggs locked him up in protective custody. But beneath the semblance of normalcy, I could feel the tension tightening, could sense the insidious infiltration of frenetic fear, the taut nerves and grim thoughts behind the masks of complacence, and I shuddered to think of what this might all be building up to.

And all this because a five year old boy was dead. Not because he was the banker's grandson, not even because he was the victim of a kidnapper. But because of they way he had died. Because of the unexplained series of parallel incisions on each side of the neck, close to the jugular veins .

* * * * * *

By nine in the evening everything was quiet. Too

quiet! Trestle, like all small towns, had an early night life of its own. Tonight the streets were practically deserted. The usual group of fellows was missing from in front of the pool room. The soda fountain in the spa was deserted, the jukebox silent. Those who ventured out, either of necessity or from sheer bravado, quickened their steps intuitively as they passed the darkened store fronts and the still darker alleyways. I'd packed away a late, hearty supper and for want of anything better to do, was relaxing on the bed in my room trying to make sense out of the problem that faced the people of Trestle.

In my travels I'd run into all kinds of superstitious folderol and always managed to laugh it off. But here, in my home town, with belief in supernatural happenings spreading by the minute, it was harder than usual to bring common sense to bear on the problem. I still felt that the whole affair must have a rational explanation.

First, the rabbits and hens that were slaughtered. I'd talked with a score of the adjacent farmers during the day. All were agreed that the toothmarks found on the blood-drained carcasses were definitely not those of an animal. The next puzzle was the weather-beaten jalopy from which I had seen the child's body drop. No one knew anyone in the entire township who owned such a car. No trace of it had been found though, even at this moment, a special posse armed with portable searchlights were probing the winding dirt roads in Devil's Swamp for some evidence it might have left the roadway to disappear in the hungry quicksand.

Finally, the body of the child, emptied of blood, with those mysterious marks at the throat. The only conclusion that seemed to fit all the facts was that the killer was a maniac, a poor deluded mind, afflicted with that dread disease, lycanthropy. If I were correct, then it might be anyone in the town or the surrounding villages. Whoever it was must be found, and soon, before the entire town went mad.

There could hardly have been a less likely moment for someone to knock at my door.

I bounded from the bed, crossed the room in long, savage strides and flung it wide. My belligerent attitude must have startled my visitor. He took a quick step or two backward while I gave him a quick once-over. He was the inoffensive, scholarly type, meekly but conservatively dressed, half a head shorter than I, and easily twenty pounds lighter. He seemed to have reached a point where years didn't matter any more. There was a note of apology in his voice.

"So sorry if I disturbed you, Mr. Dexter. I'm your next door neighbor." He indicated the room with a nod. "I . . . we . . that is we need a fourth for a friendly little game of pinochle. One of the boys said he knew you, and thought you might like to join us."

It must be someone who knew me well, and remembered that I was a card fiend from way back. Whatever the game---poker, hi-lo-jack, cribbage, rummy, anything that could be played with cards, was strictly my meat and potatoes, and more than once it had been just that!

"Sure thing, old-timer. By the way," a quick thought, "if you'll wait a minute I've got a couple of pints stashed in my suitcase . . . "

He held up a hand and shook his head .

"We have everything we need, thank you . . . except you."

It was only a moment before, door locked behind me, I was following my host across his threshold and looking at the two men who rose to greet us. One was an absolute stranger. But the other! I pounced on him like a long lost brother, and pumped his arm vigorously.

"Frank King! You old so-'n-so! You're a sight for sore eyes!"

For a couple of minutes the others must have thought it was old home week. Frank had been my buddy all through school and afterwards, right up to the time I left town. He seated me at his left. The man on my other side was introduced as Stan Miller, a newshawk Frank had met in Boston. Directly opposite me was the one who had invited me, whom Frank and the reporter addressed as "Professor."

"Whatever brought you in this direction?" Frank queried, shuffling the cards.

"Just a sudden notion. Had some time on my hands, some dough in my pockets so I yielded to an urge. Think I'll stay until after the kid's funeral."

"Good. I'll get a chance to see you at close range. I own a share in this hotel. I even work here. The day clerk takes off over the weekend, and I fill in at the desk for him."

The game turned into a see-saw affair, and after the first few hands conversation picked up again. It .was inevitable that the local situation would rear its ugly head. It was the newspaper man who brought it up with:

"Wonder what's going to happen next?"

The Professor cut himself into the talkfest for the first

time.

"If you mean what will be the vampire's next move, there's the time element to be considered. Anything may happen, tonight, tomorrow night, nothing."

I looked at him sharply. I noticed the whiteness of his hands as he held the cards, his long spatulate fingers. My response was slightly on the irritable side.

"You seem pretty darn sure about tomorrow night. How come?"

He sounded surprised that I should ask.

"Because tomorrow's Friday, of course." Then, patiently, "If you were better versed in vampire lore you would understand. Most authorities agree that Friday night and all day Saturday are allotted to the vampire for repose, and that during those hours he refrains from plying his nefarious profession."

"Are you telling me that you actually take any stock in this twiddle-twaddle?"

"Why not? It's no harder for me to believe in vampires than it would have been for your great-great-grandfather to give credence to some of the things we take for granted today."

I ran my finger beneath my collar once more. Whatever it was on the back of my neck was annoying me. I felt like asking Frank if his share of the hotel was buggy, Instead, I took some of my spite out on the Professor.

"I suppose you consider yourself an authority on such things?"

"I don't want to sound like a braggart on such short acquaintance, Mr. Dexter, but I honestly believe that I know more about vampires than any man living."

You can't kill a man for blowing his own horn, but there was something about this little guy that riled me. I snapped at him like a mud turtle.

"And just who on earth might you be?

His eyes blinked through his horned-rimmed spectacles.

"I had forgotten you didn't know me. I'm Mr. Smith, a student of occult phenomena, with special reference to vampires. I've been retained by Mr. George Webster to bring my particular talents to bear in the present investigation. You have as much right to be skeptical as I have to be otherwise but, before I leave town, I'd like an opportunity to convince you that vampires are more than a mere figment of one's imagination."

This could have gone on for hours if the room telephone hadn't interrupted. The Professor rose to answer it.

"John Charles Smith speaking . . . yes . . . of course . . . it's for you," as he handed the receiver to Miller.

"What? You don't say? That'll keep the story alive. Be right over."

He turned to us, excitement in his eyes.

"Double trouble. They found where the car went off the road in Devil's Swamp. And right here in town, six men wearing sheets over-powered the sexton and raised havoc in the church graveyard. They dug up a couple of recently buried bodies, broke open the caskets, and chopped off the heads with their spades!"

* * * * * * *

All four of us went in Stan Miller's car. I sat in front

with the reporter, and Frank climbed in back with the Professor. I couldn't resist confiding to Stan that the old man's ideas impressed me as being a little on the crackpot side.

"Maybe his ideas are a little screwy, Pete, but lots of people go for them. He's come to be quite well known around Boston, giving lectures on ghosts, werewolves, vampires, and all that kind of rot. Personally, I think the whole business is a lot of tripe, but it's a free country, and if folks want to fall for his line that's their business."

The churchyard was only a few blocks away. It looked like about half the town had reached the place ahead of us. Miller's press card and the Professors' credentials finally got us through the police line. The serenity of the little cemetery was gone. The ghouls had made a shambles of the place. Headstones were overturned, well kept graves were trampled and desecrated. Pieces of splintered coffins were strewn haphazardly about the place. And the pitiful, decapitated remains of the exhumed! The gruesome, severed heads with their sightless sockets! I shivered. John Charles Smith volunteered in heartfelt sympathy:

"It was all so unnecessary. Anyone should have known that these poor souls were not vampires."

The sexton was closely questioned. How many men were there? How were they dressed? Did he recognize any of them by build, mannerisms, voice?

He knew very little. He had been in his cottage between the church and the graveyard when he heard the commotion. He came out at once. There were at least half a dozen men. Each was clad in a sheet-like garment with holes to see through. It was a simple matter for them to overpower him and bind and gag him with strips of the same material from which the costumes were made. How did the police hear of it before even more damage had been done? He didn't know the answer to that one.

They found that out from the mother of a girl who had passed the churchyard on her way home from the movies. She saw the eerie figures, and ran the rest of the way home screaming of ghosts in the graveyard. In normal times her mother would have laughed it off as something the child dreamed up. Things being as they were she had phoned the police. The girl's frightened cries must have warned the marauders for by the time the police arrived, all of them had fled.

Stan Miller decided he had vacuumed every possible bit of news from the scene, glanced at his watch, announced his deadline was still a few hours away, and invited us to ride along with him while he checked the other story.

The ride into Devil's Swamp held a horror of its own. A thick haze hung over everything. It was impossible to see more than a few feet ahead on the rutted, stony roads. The weird call of night birds accentuated the spooky atmosphere. This whole business was beginning to get under my skin. I glanced back at the Professor. He sat there as unconcerned as though the sun was high in the heavens and we were speeding along a modern macadam highway. Had the man no nerves, or was he drawing his strength from entities which peopled the swamp, outre beings which the rest of us could neither see nor hear?

We were halted at one of the forks in the road, the

only point where there was a clearing large enough to turn the car. We went the rest of the way on foot. The only illumination was the brave beam of Stan's flashlight as it struggled to cut through the thickening fog.

There was not too much to see when we finally reached the spot. Just the grim evidence of tire marks showing that a car, traveling at high speed, had skidded and left the road. Frank picked up a stone. He tossed it beyond the point where the wheel marks vanished. We watched while the deadly sands gripped it and silently sucked it from our sight.

The Trestle Diner was still open when we reached town. I had Stan drop me off while he headed for a 'phone to shoot through his story. I'd eaten a big supper but I was still hungry, and I smacked my lips over a couple of hamburgers, two cups of java, and a big hunk of cherry pie.

Back at the hotel I should have dropped off into a dreamless sleep. I'm the last one in the world to be troubled with insomnia. But I tossed and turned, and tried to marshall my thoughts into semblance of a reasonable argument as to why I did not believe in vampires. No goofy Professor was going to outtalk me when we had our get-together.

To begin with, nothing had happened in Trestle so far that couldn't be explained by natural means. Vampires were as much a myth as the legendary gods of ancient Greece or the fantastic tales of Sinbad the Sailor. They were the products of ignorance and fear, of the inability of people to explain phenomena beyond the scope of the sciences of their day and age. It was like the caveman's blind worship of fire until he chained it and made it do his bidding.

And there were other so-called mysteries that had

logical explanations. Before our modern embalming methods many people were buried alive. Groans were often heard from their tombs, as they struggled to escape from their horrendous doom. Bodies were found to have turned in their graves, shrouds torn, cheeks fresh, eyes open and staring, limbs contorted in grotesque positions. Or if a woman two-timed her husband, what more logical excuse than that she was set upon by an incubus, that the child she eventually bore was conceived by a vampire!

Wizards, witches, werewolves, one cursed by his parents or the church---even suicides---all were supposed at death to become vampires, being neither ghosts nor demons, neither dead nor alive, doomed forever to prey upon their fellow men and sustain themselves by drinking the blood from the veins of living human beings. In addition, every victim of a vampire's bite was supposed to become a vampire. The whole thing was a mathematical impossibility!

I remembered reading somewhere recently that in the United States alone, there were almost twenty thousand suicides a year! If each one of these marked only one man, woman or child for its victim, and each victim was likewise impelled to seek another, it wouldn't be long before everyone in the world would be a vampire, and there'd be no one left to prey upon! The vicious breed would die from starvation. Let's see the Professor talk his way out of that one!

I don't know exactly when I dropped off to sleep I do know that my dreams were filled with malevolent beings with faces like death masks, stretching out scrawny arms, trying to clutch my clothing with sharp, curved nails, fang-like teeth seeking to plunge into the softness of my throat where my veins stood out like beacons and throbbed until my head was splitting with the pain of it all.

I still thought I was dreaming when I opened my eyes. It was a full minute before I realized that the stench of a fresh-opened grave in my nostrils was not part and parcel of my nightmare. My fingers sought my neck of their own volition, and came away wet, and red, and sticky!

Some one, or some thing had been in my room, had left so recently that the putrescent odor of its presence still hung heavy in the air.

I was sure that I hadn't made a sound. The shock of what had occurred had left me voiceless. Yet I'd hardly sensed what had happened before I heard a faint tapping on my door and the voice of the Professor calling.

"Mr. Dexter . . . Mr. Dexter . . . is anything wrong?"

For the second time that night I opened the door to him. This time he entered without invitation, and indulged in a deep, audible inhalation. He crossed the room, leaned out of the window, glanced right and left, recrossed the room and began a minute examination of the lock on the door. I sat upon the edge of the bed and caught a bit of his soliloquy.

"A two-story drop . . . a man could make it in safety . . but there's no possible way he could climb to the window . . . the lock's in perfect working order . . . " Then, addressing his remarks directly to me: "Tell me about it. What happened? All your impressions. "

I told him, even including my nightmarish dreams. He examined my neck, not only the fresh wound but also the spot on the other side which had irritated me all through the day. He shook his head, squinted at me through his horn-rimmed glasses. His face took on a sage expression.

He questioned me some more.

Did I wake up yesterday morning feeling as though I was all in? Had I suddenly developed a craving for food, well above my normal appetite, especially for meats? Had I felt the urge for something to drink that even liquor could not seem to satisfy?

I replied in the negative to his last query and he seemed to be less agitated.

"It's lucky for you I knew of this in time. Another day might have been too late! Now it is Friday, there will be no danger. I think everything will work out all right."

I still couldn't orient myself to his way of thinking. Neither could I understand my resentment of him. I was baffled, more than a trifle overwrought.

"What on earth are you driving at, Smith? Too late for what? Or is all this a part of my dream?"

"You're as wide awake as you've ever been in your life, my friend. I know it will take more than mere words of mine to convince you, but you have had a caller these past two nights, an uninvited guest who has nourished himself at the expense of your eternal soul! It's entirely up to me. There is nothing you can do about it now." He checked his wrist watch. "It's only three o'clock. Go back to sleep. He will not bother you again, now. Eat hearty, tomorrow and regain some of the vitality he has drawn from you. I shall trap him before too many days!"

He was talking like a blithering idiot. A crazy man! Of course he couldn't convince me. Did he think I was a complete fool? I had a different idea.

"Maybe you're the vampire. How do I know? You were back at the hotel ahead of me. Your room is right next to mine. There was no key in the door then. You could have tampered with the lock, fixed it so you could get in. You could have cut my neck and filled the room with noxious perfume. It's too pat to suit me, your being right outside the door before I'd fully awakened. I've had more than enough of this vampire hokum for one session. You'd better get back to your room before I really lose my temper!"

He gave me a long, meaningful stare, seemed satisfied with what he read in my eyes and left without another word. I made sure that the door was securely fastened, closed and bolted the window, and crawled back under the covers to sleep soundly until the sun was high.

* * * * * * *

By the time I'd had breakfast it was mid-morning. I woke up with such a big head I even opened my suitcase and looked at the two unopened pints to convince myself I hadn't been on a private binge. I felt nervous and touchy. I hoped nobody would rub my fur the wrong way until I regained control of myself.

In the dining room of the hotel I caught myself casting overt glances at the other patrons, noticing one with hairy hands, another with pointed ears, still another with long, sharp fingernails. That last was somewhat of a laugh. As long as there were manicurists like Myrna, well-bred people would have pointed nails !

I wondered why I had thought of Myrna. I chuckled. The real wonder was why I hadn't thought of her. I looked at my own hands. Maybe I should keep the promise I made to myself and drop over that way. As I recalled her full red lips and whistle-stop figure, it seemed like a very sensible idea.

I knew that last night's episode in my room had not been imagination. Imagination wouldn't have left a scabbed-over cut on my neck that I wanted to scratch all the time. I regretted my flare-up at the little Professor. It was silly to think that he was capable of whatever it was that had happened to me. I owed him an apology. I'd see he got it next time we met.

When I stopped at the desk to leave my room key I even gave the clerk who had checked me in a more than passing scrutiny. My mind registered his saturnine face, his wan complexion, his thick hands with their pudgy fingers. I wondered if he . . . .

I caught myself up short. If I didn't watch out, I'd have myself believing in this vampire hocus-pocus, too.

At long last I was once more on the street mingling with the crown. Everyone was talking about the news of the night before. As usual, opinions were sharply divided. Some frankly supported the masked men who had invaded the churchyard; others condemned them, calling for their identification and punishment. As for the evidence that the jalopy I'd seen had been swallowed up forever by Devil's Swamp, this too, brought disagreement. Some felt that the kidnapper had perished inside the vanished car. Others, that no vampire could be trapped that way and that, even now, he was searching out new victims. Truly, Trestle was a town in turmoil. Of such contradictory opinions, such wild imaginings, such growing convictions, is trouble brewed.

My subconscious mind apparently never lost sight of

the fact that I was heading for a manicure. My meanderings slowly but surely brought me to Joe's door. Today there was no waiting line, there were no customers in the chairs. Joe looked worried. He seemed honestly happy to see me.

"Hi ya, Pete. You must be a mind reader. I was just wondering how I could catch up with you. I need a little help, and you're just the man for the job."

"S'matter, Joe, run out of hair tonic?"

"No, Pete, this is serious. It's about the girl who works for me . . . you know, the manicurist. She nicked one of the boys yesterday, and because she made a fuss over the guy and bandaged up his finger, he's got the crazy idea that she's the vampire---either her, or her grandfather, that nobody in town ever sees. He's making a big story out of it. I'm afraid some of these young squirts are just hotheaded enough to pull some rotten stunt like those fellows did up at the graveyard last night. Right now things around here are dry as tinder, and one spark might set off something that all the cops in the county couldn't control."

"You know me, Joe. If there's anything I can do to help . . . ."

"There is. First of all, though, I want you to meet the girl. Myrna, come out for a minute. This is Pete Dexter, the one I was telling you about."

She acknowledged the introduction with a smile that could have demanded any red-blooded guy to do anything she wanted. I was wondering what she might want me to do when Joe Parker broke into my reverie .

"Here's what I've got in mind. I already told you Myrna lives alone with her granddad in Dodson's old shack up by Salem Woods. There's nobody anywhere around she can call on in case of trouble. Mame and I thought 'twould be a good idea if they moved in with us 'till this blows over. I can't leave the shop alone or I'd do it myself. Ken Davis is waiting in front of the bank with his station wagon. You remember Ken? I nodded. "What I want you to do is to go there with him and the girl and help get the old gent down to my place. Okay?"

"Roger! When do we start?"

"Right now, if you're both ready. I'll 'phone Mame to be looking for you."

It was only about three blocks from Joe's shop to the First National Bank. We didn't hurry---at least, I didn't. I was enjoying my company. Even as much as Myrna monopolized my attention, I had the feeling that many eyes were watching us every step of the way. It sent little tingles of anticipation up and down my spine. It was a long time since I'd had a chance to be in the thick of things, and though I didn't want any harm to come to either the girl or her grandfather, I was yearning for action.

Davis was waiting. We crowded in to the front seat with him. Not that I minded the crowding part of it, with Myrna Simmons acting as the in-between! About the only way Ken had changed was to grow older, still the cheery, roly-poly type that had to jam a little to fit behind the wheel. I hoped the other things I remembered about him were equally true . . that he was calm when there was trouble, liked a scrap as well as I did, packed a terrific wallop and had the weight behind it to make something. He didn't recognize me, so Myrna had to introduce us.

"Hope we make it in time," he confided. "It don't look so good to me. The boys have been getting together, two or three at a time, ever since I've been waiting here. Think they meant to wait until night, but now they've seen us head out towards the woods, they might decide to speed things up a little. If we can make Mame's we'll be all right, 'cause she can 'phone for help the minute they start anything."

We made the shack in real good time, considering the shape that old station wagon was in. When I saw the dilapidated condition of the ancient building I couldn't understand how Myrna Simmons could even bear to go into the place, let alone live there.

Inside, though, everything was neat as a new pin, so clean you wouldn't mind if you had to eat off the floor. The girl's grandfather lay on a comfortable bed in the sunniest of the three rooms, his legs and arms drawn all out of shape, pitiful and helpless. A wheel chair stood in one corner. It took time and considerable care to move the frail body, first into the wheel chair and then ease both into the station wagon. When we were finally able to pull away, it was growing dark.

We were about half way to Joe's home when it happened, at the only spot along the road where side roads cut right and left and deep gullies lined both sides of the highway. The whole place was suddenly alive with cars and people. There must have been half-a-hundred men in the mob. They forced the station wagon to the edge of the road and surrounded it. They were armed with anything they had been able to lay their hands on---clubs, shovels, hammers, hoe handles, stones. Their faces were flaming with frenzy, the mad unreasoning frenzy of a mob, where might is right, and nothing else matters.

I hopped out of the station wagon. Myrna scrambled over the seat into the body of the vehicle, where her grandfather waited in the wheel chair. Davis squirmed out from under the wheel and launched himself into the fray. I knew it was going to be a tough battle . My whole object was to fight my way around to the back before any of them succeeded in battering in the rear door. If it hadn't been for their improvised weapons, I'd have made it easily. As it was, I was doing okay. I'd just about reached the corner of the car when I heard two clearly distinguishable sounds: the crash of the door as it gave way, and the distant shrieking of sirens.

I looked up to see Myrna standing on the floor of the station wagon, her arms thrown wide to protect the invalid behind her. Just then a stone hurled by one of the crowd struck her full in the face and blood flowed freely.

I think I went berserk at that moment. I fought with the fury of a madman. All the while the sound of sirens was drawing nearer. I must have been about fifty feet away before realization broke over me with all its horror-filled implications. My frantic urge to reach Myrna Simmons was not prompted by my desire to save her from bodily harm. It was the rich, red blood still running down her white cheek---an overpowering, all compelling desire to moisten my parched lips with it; better yet, to drink my fill!

Was all this business about vampires true, after all? Was I actually one of the foul breed? Was it a figment of my madness, or did I see the Professor coming up fast from the fringe of the diminishing crowd? I was slugging it out with one of the boys right at the edge of the highway, on the brink of the deep, stone-lined gully. I may have slipped and dived head first onto the stones. I may have been tripped and clouted over the head. Either way, the result was the same. Swift, sure, complete blackout!

* * * * * * *

I was lying at the bottom of the gully when I opened my eyes. My head felt as if seventeen devils were battering the inside of my skull with sledge hammers. I dug my fingers into my palms and choked back a groan. The pounding subsided a bit and my blurred vision cleared enough for me to identify the man bending over me as John Charles Smith. He offered me a welcomed hand. With his help, I made it to my feet, and together we started up the steep slope to the highway. His strength and agility surprised me. I decided I must have been way off when I guessed at his age. We finally made it.

The road was deserted except for the Professor and me. No crowd. No station wagon. No Ken. No. Myrna. Not even a car in sight. And I got the impression that there was an important difference, one I had not yet fully grasped because of my befuddled condition. The scene that met my eyes bore all the familiar contours of the countryside where I was born and reared, yet I had the same tense feeling that always swept over me whenever I set foot on foreign ground.

The Professor must have read my mind .

"I don't wonder that you're mystified. Things have been piling up mighty fast. You're both right and wrong. You're still in Trestle, yet you're not in Trestle. You're in America, yet you're not in America. Actually, you are in Murania. You are now in my world. "

I'm here, I'm not here! If I'm not here I must be somewhere else! But I'm not somewhere else so I must be here! You sound like a broken-down burlesque comic. Cut the double talk. I suppose the next thing you'll try to tell me is that I'm not me."

"I must insist, Mr. Dexter, that you calm down and take me seriously. Facts are facts and must be faced sooner or later. The simplest way is to give me a chance to prove what I'm saying. This is the same planet, the same earth, where you were so valiantly defending yourself but a few moments ago. But, with the same degree of definiteness, I repeat that you are in a different world."

I must still have shown my incredulity, for he continued:

"The idea of co-existent universes is not new. Perhaps you will understand it more quickly if I use a simple analogy. You are familiar with radio and television. You know that scores of programs are being broadcast simultaneously on different wave lengths, yet not one interferes with any other. Unless you are tuned to the right station you hear nothing except the usual sounds of everyday living. You know that radio is a fact, therefore you believe it. Otherwise it would seem to you like the wild dream of an opium addict. The same is true of your video channels, only here you have pictures as well as sound."

Fantastic as the idea was, it made sense the way he told it. I nodded my acquiescence.

"The same thing is also true of all life forms. The world you live in is peopled with countless other parallel existences, each completely unconscious of the other, yet separated only by an infinitesimal differential as yet unfathomed by man. Few have the power to cross from their universe into one of the co-existent ones; none can ever explore them all, for their number is infinite. As I told you before, this is Murania, named from a word the Bohemians of your land used to designate my people. This, Mr. Pete Dexter, is the Vampire Empire!"

He removed his horn-rimmed glasses. His nimble fingers extracted a tiny screwdriver from his vest pocket. For a second he looked directly at me and I could feel the hypnotic power in his deep set, beady eyes. As he talked, he made minute adjustments in the screws that held the hinges together.

"You must realize by now that you are here with me because you are temporarily one of us. Otherwise I could never have brought you across the borderline. I have brought you here for an emergency treatment so that you, who have involuntarily become a blood brother, need not be permanently affected."

He replaced his spectacles, drew a duplicate pair from an inside pocket, and began his delicate adjustment of the screws.

"There is no time to lose. You must be treated as soon as possible. Furthermore, I must be back in your world promptly, so that I may complete the job to which I have been assigned. We must go at once to the nearest center, which corresponds geographically to Boston in world you know. "

In the deepening twilight, the trees became ghostly guardians of the deserted highway.

"You have noted the absence of vehicles. We do not

need them here. For long distances we travel by teleportation." He handed me the second pair of glasses. Once more his eyes bored into mine. "Put them on. I have tuned them to the area for which we are headed. It will only make it harder for both of us if you resist. Place your hands on my shoulders, hold tight, and look into my eyes."

My senses swam under his penetrating gaze. I swear I could not have counted up to five before he dropped his eyes and I could see clearly once more.

We were standing on what I judged to be the lower end of Washington Street, but a Washington Street such as I had never seen. It was lined on both sides with tomb-like structures of varying sizes. Each was of alabaster whiteness with the texture of fine marble. The larger buildings reminded me of overgrown mausoleums. Some of these were severely plain, others were ornately decorated with bas-reliefs of exquisite workmanship. It was as though I had been transplanted into a mammoth cemetery that extended for miles in every direction.

But, if it looked like a cemetery, the hum of activity gave the lie to the comparison. The place was alive with action. The street was filled with people of all descriptions, men and women who looked little different from those I had always known. Darkness was closing in, and the buildings glowed faintly with an eerie fluorescence that cast an unreal air over the scene. John Charles hurried me through the throng, talking all the while. It was like one of those guided tours they have in the bigger cities. He pointed out one of the larger buildings.

This is the receiving center. We have one in operation

to match every large city in our world. To these centers, after burial, are brought those whose life or manner of death condemn them to lustful unrest. Here they go through the first stages of our indoctrination. There are many who do not respond, the sorcerers, the devotees of black magic, the wizards and witches of this modern age. After a prescribed period, these are summarily eliminated."

I was trying to readjust myself to this aspect of vampirism. It was so different from anything I had formerly heard, or the things that most people believed. My guide seemed to anticipate the questions forming in my mind.

"Legend is a curious admixture of fact and fancy. In the case of the vampire, so many different crimes have been laid at his door it is particularly difficult to sift out the true from the false. Every country, every nation, has its own set of superstitions. Of them all, the Bulgarians hit closest to the truth. They believed that, after a forty-day apprenticeship in the world of shadows, a vampire could successfully pass himself off as a normal human being with none of the usual outward attributes by which it is said we may be recognized. We find a much longer time must elapse before we can safely appear among you. At least two years intensive training is required in our special schools before any are granted permission to cross into your world.

"For centuries, only the victim of a vampire's bite, or he whose corpse was crossed by a cat or a bird before burial, was classed as an involuntary vampire. But since the Church abandoned its recognition of us, suicides now fall into the same category. We are in the majority here. We make our laws. We have our courts, our judges, our executioners. Our theology is much the same as it was in life. This is our Purgatory, the place where our souls can be cleansed of our vicious desires in preparation for the hereafter. Because of our affliction, we cannot have churches, crosses, or any such thing in evidence here. We have dedicated our twenty-year term of expiation to protect humanity from the more pernicious of our species."

He turned in at one of the larger buildings and gestured for me to follow. To the uniformed guard who halted us at the entrance he said: "John Charles Smith, V.B.I." and turned back the lapel of his coat to expose some insignia to the man's gaze.

My first impression was that we were in a large chemical workshop. More than a hundred men and women were working at benches or monitoring huge, thoroughly automatic machines. Again the Professor caught my thought and answered my unspoken question.

"One of the most important things in any world is the problem of sustenance for its inhabitants. Ours was a rather difficult one. We must have blood to satisfy our unholy appetite. We created and successfully used the blood bank for generations, and kept its secrets to ourselves till we no longer needed it. Some of the keenest minds the world has ever known have been suicides and we have benefitted by their knowledge. Eventually a chemical compound was perfected that contained all the components of rich, human blood. Exhaustive tests were worked out by which the exact dose required for each individual vampire could be determined.

"These rations are issued monthly, and periodic check-ups are required. Once in a great while, more often in European countries than here, someone escapes our vigilance by simulating satisfaction with our synthetic diet and, as soon as he is able, eludes us. It is then our job to apprehend him before too much damage has been done. It is such a mission which turned my steps toward Trestle."

We came to the end of the block-long building and made our exit to Tremont Street. The sun had set, and with the increasing darkness the illumination radiating from the buildings had intensified in brilliance so that everything around us was as bright as day. John Charles pointed to an edifice just across the way.

"At last we have reached our objective, Mr. Dexter. It is where we bring all emergency cases. Right this way, please."

It looked for all the world like the clinic of a large hospital. Smith nodded at the pleasant-faced receptionist, and led me through a labyrinth of narrow passageways, past trim-clad nurses and white-coated interns, finally swinging into a space equipped with all the usual appurtenances of an accident room. He identified himself briefly to the doctor in charge.

"John Charles Smith, V.B.I. Emergency case. Attacked two night in succession. No evidence of previous attacks. Usual treatment, please!" Again he turned back his coat lapel. This time I caught a fleeting glimpse of a blood-red, bat shaped pin .

I removed coat and shirt at the doctor's request. He made a cursory examination of the marks on my neck and throat, while the efficient nurse busied herself setting the stage.

The innoculation you are to be given," Smith explained, "is quite similar in purpose to the Pasteur treatment. It should take effect immediately. By the time I have returned you to your own sphere the effects of your unpleasant experience will be completely nullified."

For the first time since my arrival in this strange city I found my tongue.

"This whole darn set up knocks me for a loop. I think you've made everything clear to me except one thing. What the devil does 'V.B.I." stand for?"

The Professor hesitated, then spoke.

"There's no good reason why I shouldn't tell you. I think there will be just about time while you are being innoculated. I was a college professor in California before overwork undermined my health and I decided to end it all. As I told you, a two-year training period here is compulsory. At the end of that time we are allowed to volunteer for any sort of service consistent with our physical and mental capabilities.

"I applied for assignment to the Vampire Bureau of Investigation, and my request was granted. It meant another three years of hard work and intensive study before I won my right to return to the world from whence I came. As is customary, I was assigned to the opposite end of the country to avoid possible recognition, for no one must suspect our true status, or our usefulness is ended. For the past fifteen years I have been one of the hundreds of us who labor among you. My record was an exemplary one until one of the souls I had helped across the border failed to respond to our methods and fled. All V.B.I.'s in America were alerted, but he was held to be my special responsibility. For three long months we were unable to find him. When the Webster boy disappeared we felt that it was our first tangible clue. I left immediately for Trestle. This, Mr. Dexter, is my final assignment. If I can carry it to a successful conclusion I will be able to claim the right to pass on to my eternal reward."

It was just at that moment that the doctor pressed the plunger of the hypodermic needle in his hand. I've had hypos before, plenty of them, but that one packed the kick of a mule. The room spun like a top. The doctor's face became as big as a mountain, and there were ten of him where only one should be. The spinning room increased its tempo until all became a dizzying blur. Once more, unconsciousness claimed me.

* * * * * * *

I felt every bit as rocky as the ground on which I was lying. It took a lot of effort, but I struggled to a sitting position to sort of take inventory. I could hear the hum of tires as an occasional car whizzed past on the roadway above me. It was country black. If you've ever wakened at the bottom of a gully, after sunset, on a moonless night, several miles from the nearest town, you'll know exactly what I mean.

It was a glorious scrap, but I was sure I'd carry mementoes of it for several days. My head felt like an elephant had trampled on it and I was having more than a little trouble opening my right eye. I felt the back of my head gingerly. It was lumpy as a bride's first batch of mashed potatoes. The hair was matted with nearly-dried blood in several places. My clothes were dirty and torn. All in all, I looked a mess.

I sat there for a few minutes to get some of my

strength back and began to wonder about a few things. How long I'd been out. What happened to Myrna and her grandfather. Why everyone had gone off and left me unconscious at he bottom of the gully. If I had really seen John Charles Smith coming towards me as I plunged headlong. If I had, where was he now? Had I been riding a nightmare or was there actually such a place as Murania? I felt a sudden twinge of pain in my right arm, and the fingers of my left hand sought out the spot. It was too dark to see, but it was just the kind of soreness that would be left by the jab of a needle. Then I began to wonder how I was going to make it back to Trestle. I hadn't hitch-hiked since the time I was stranded in Australia. I wondered if I'd forgotten the technique.

It was a slow and painful process, but I finally made the grade back to the highway. My legs still wobbly, my whole body stiff and sore, I started on the tiresome trek to town.

The first dozen drivers ignored my extended thumb like I was a leper. I don't know as I blamed them much. I must have looked like a drunken stumble-bum, as I weaved along the road.

A car coming from Trestle passed me, pulled over to the shoulder. Someone honked the horn vigorously. I turned and hobbled in its direction. Opened doors disgorged three men, who hurried toward me---the trio of the pinochle game . . the reporter, Frank King, and the Professor. Did I imagine it or did he touch his finger to his lips as a warning to keep silent? As if I'd say anything to them about Murania! They'd think I was more nutty than Lem Settle!

"Where've you been? What happened? You look like

you've been through a threshing machine!"

"Last I remember I was mixing it up at the edge of the road. All of a sudden . . . blooey! The way my head feels, I think somebody zapped me. When I woke up a few minutes ago I was at the bottom of the gully."

Stan and Frank eased me into the back seat and I sat back with a sigh of relief.

I suddenly thought to ask, "How come you were headed in this direction?"

"Looking for you. When the cops came to the rescue, everybody beat it except the ones you and Ken knocked for a loop. When Davis got ready to pull away he looked for you. When he didn't see you he figured you'd finagled a ride in one of the police cars. When you didn't turn up either at Joe's or at the hotel we decided to come out and look for you. The Professor said he could show us exactly where the fight occurred, so we brought him along. How do you feel?"

"Don't worry about me, Frank. Give me a good night's rest and a piece of raw beef for my eye, and tomorrow you'll never know it happened. I'd like to get my hands on the guy who conked me on the bean!"

The Professor, in the front seat with Stan Miller, squirmed uneasily. So he was the one! Was it because that was the only way he could snatch an opportunity to take me into his world without anyone realizing that we had gone? But, had we gone? If I admitted that, I must also admit that John Charles Smith had convinced me. That I knew he was a vampire! That I conceded he had saved me from the tragedy of a similar fate. More than anything else at that moment I wanted to examine the hinges of his horn-rimmed spectacles, to turn back the lapel of his coat and look for a blood red, bat-shaped symbol. I swayed dizzily. Frank's voice sounded miles away.

"Pete . . . What's wrong? There . . . that's better! Thought you were going to pass out on me."

"I'm okay, now. The reaction, I guess."

I settled back in silence for the rest of the ride. The town had spent itself in this last spree. Everything was quiet, again. But the tension was still there. So was the vile being from beyond the grave. The thing which for two nights had singled me out for its prey. A fugitive from a co-existent world. A miscreant from Murania.

I called Joe from the pay phone in the hotel. Everything was fine. Myrna and her grandfather were safely ensconced in his home. The stone-cut on Myrna's face? Deep, but not jagged. All you could see of it now was a band-aid. Mame didn't even think it would leave a scar. Was I all right? I was? Fine! They'd all see me tomorrow.

The Professor left while I was in the booth and left a message that I'd hear from him later. I knew I must be a sight and tried to maneuver so that Stan and Frank concealed me as much as possible as they helped me across the hotel lobby. I glanced at the clock. Eight forty-five? It seemed like midnight after all I'd been through these last few hours. The boys stayed with me till I'd climbed the stairs and negotiated the length of the hall to my room. Frank promised to send up sandwiches and coffee. A hot bath on the outside, lunch on the inside, and I felt a hundred percent better.

A sensible man would have gone right to bed, but there are many times when I simply can't be sensible. Instead, I dressed in clean clothes from the skin out. I had the feeling that my activities for the day were far from ended. I propped up my pillows, sat back on the bed, lighted my pipe, and waited.

* * * * * * *

The clock on the town hall was striking ten when the Professor rapped on my door. He did not seem the least bit surprised because I was dressed and waiting. Tonight he was brisk efficiency. He outlined rapidly and precisely what he had already done, and what he wanted me to do. I listened carefully.

"It's all right if you're sure you've got the right man. But if you've made a mistake . . ."

"I am John Charles Smith. In matters such as these I make no errors. Be sure to complete your task and be back here well before one. We must strike at the witching hour."

I found the good Father of the little Catholic Church not only very cooperative but also a great deal more conversant with the subject of vampirism than I anticipated. He told me of many forms of exorcism practised by the priests in European countries, and evidenced concern lest it be found that any of his parishioners had taken part either in the graveyard episode or the attack on Myrna Simmons and her helpless grandfather. He expressed his relief when I assured him that the two had escaped unscathed. He even helped me solve my other problem. He drove me to that part of Devil's Swamp where he recalled having seen the buckthorn I wanted, and held his flashlight for me while I gathered enough for my needs .

Smith was waiting for me. Once more he went over

the details of the part I was to play in the coming drama. He was without his eyeglasses, in shirt sleeves, and had doffed his shoes. I removed mine at his suggestion, but decided my coat pockets would be needed for the things I would have to use.

We tiptoed up the two flights of stairs to the top floor. An excited youth with fire-red hair awaited us in the shadows.

"I've been right on the job, Mr. Smith," he whispered. "After he got through work, he didn't eat any supper or nothin', just come upstairs an' went in his room. I've been keepin' my eyes glued to that door ever since, but there ain't nobody gone in or out all night."

"Good work, son." I saw a bill change hands. "Keep watching, and if anybody comes upstairs who doesn't belong here, try to hold him off until we finish."

We stole silently to the last room at the end of the long hall, the room directly above the one I occupied two floors below. The Professor fished a small tool from his pants pocket, inserted it into the old-fashioned lock with the utmost care and slowly, soundlessly turned the key that locked the door from the inside. With equal caution he eased open the door. We inched our way in, testing every step, fearful of creaking boards. The air of the room was foul and fetid, with the same obscene smell I had detected in my room the night before.

* * * * * * *

Spotlighted by the shaft of brilliant moonlight that fell plumb center on the bed, arms folded across his chest, lay the one we were seeking. Stretched at full length, stiff and rigid as a corpse, he was totally unaware of our presence. His blood red lips, his face contorted in a mask of indefinable evil, belied his seeming repose. It was as if some strange power held in check his demoniac desires, made him powerless to carry out his iniquitous appetences. For a moment I almost failed to recognize him as the day clerk at the Mansion House.

I also almost neglected the job I had promised to perform. John Charles Smith was already tracing a large imaginary circle completely around the bed to the accompaniment of a chant in some unintelligible ancient tongue. I turned first to the door we had just entered. Over the knob I draped a crucifix through which had been looped a pliant branch of buckthorn. I hung a similar one over the latch of the single window. Withdrawing into the shadows near the bed I opened the wide-mouthed jar I carried. Smith completed his incantation. He crossed to the bed, reached out, shook the shoulder of the sleeper.

"Sam . . . Sam Denison . . . wake up . . . wake up . . . "

The body stirred uneasily. The Professor renewed his efforts. He turned the full power of his hypnotic gaze upon the immobile form. As if drawn by some irresistible force the body slowly . . . oh, so slowly . . . came to a sitting position. The eyelids fluttered, lifted. Never in all my lifetime have I seen such abysmal putridness, such unspeakable corruption as mirrored in those malefic eyes. The legs drew up suddenly. The creature gathered for a spring. Smith raised an arm. At the signal, I flung the contents of the jar at the attacker. The stream of liquid struck him full on the neck and shoulders.

His shriek was that of a soul in torment. Just two words, repeated, as he sank back on the bed, his whole frame shaking with anguished sobs.

"I burn . . . I burn . . . I burn . . . "

Smith stepped to the bed once more. I saw the glint of moonlight on metal as the Professor plunged a needle into the cringing being. The cries subsided to a piteous mewling.

"The medication I have given you serves a double purpose. It will alleviate the burning of the holy water, and will make it impossible for you to lie to me. You cannot escape. There is a crucifix both at the door and at the window. You know me. You know that I have the power to exorcise you completely. But this, right now, I must not do. You have broken the laws of not one world, but two. First you must pay your debt to the society of the land to which you chose to return. Now, Sam Denison, I want the whole story."

The eyes of John Charles Smith never left his captive's face. When Denison spoke it was in the halting manner of one in a trance.

"When I escaped from Murania I had a month's supply of capsules with me. My indoctrination had progressed so far I could not overcome my repugnance against actually attacking a living human being. Instead, I sought the hospitals, worked for awhile, rifled the blood banks. The money I earned piled up. There was nothing I needed to spend it for but clothes. I learned of this job at the hotel through an employment agency. It seemed ideal for my purposes, even to having Friday night and all day Saturday off. I spent most of the money I had for that old jalopy, and kept it parked in the woods off Lincoln Road.

"It worked out beautifully. With the car, I could go far afield, and prey on small animals with which the woods abound, supplementing them with an occasional foray on a nearby farm.

"All my life I had longed to travel, to see this world of ours, but fate had always kept me penniless, chained to a life I hated. That's why I turned on the gas in my rooming house to end it all, and you transported me to Murania. But I left, because I wanted money, lots of it, so I could satisfy my yearnings. When I kidnapped the Webster boy I meant to hold him for ransom. Once in my hands, the money would take me to foreign shores. I reasoned that no one would suspect a mere hotel clerk of being involved in such a crime. Nor would anyone dream that the missing boy was right here in this room, right in the center of town. I had no thought of harming him.

"Once I had him here, helpless, desire became stronger than reason. He was so young, his flesh so tender, his blood so rich and pure. When he died I became panicky. I intended to dispose of the body in the quicksands. You know how my plans miscarried. After I got rid of the car it took me all night to make my way back to the hotel without being apprehended. I made it by a margin of minutes before I went on duty for the day.

"I decided that to run away would be the worst thing I could do. I must sit tight, at least till the hue and cry had died down. I knew, also, that from now on, substitutes would never again satisfy me. And, in a hotel where guests were constantly changing, there was no danger that I would ever starve!"

His head bowed in resignation, John Charles Smith allowed himself a satisfied sigh.

"I took Frank into my confidence this morning. We

planted the microphone, and rigged up the wire recorder which, even now, he must be playing back in my room to the county detective. If the rest of my instructions were followed, the police are waiting outside the door.

"Some of Sam Denison's story will be neither understood nor believed, but his confession will hold. The general public may class him as a homicidal maniac. It may be better for the peace of mind of the people of Trestle if they do think so. New England justice is swift and sure, and this time there will be no release from the grave. I will not have too long to wait before my last assignment is completed!

"And now, Pete Dexter, if you will kindly remove that crucifix from the doorknob, I will deliver this gentleman to the proper authorities. You must have forgotten that, so long as that object remains there, I am as much a prisoner in this room as he!"

A Solitary Solution

THE FUNERAL OF JOSIAH KEENE was over, but the big house was still shrouded in an atmosphere of gloomy depression. Now that the many friends of the dead man had gone and the old mansion was silent once more, the impression of somber dreariness was accentuated a hundred-fold.

This all had its effect on the quintet that gathered in the old-fashioned parlor where but a few hours before the casket of the dead man lay; indeed, the housekeeper, the only woman among them, cast apprehensive glances at the spot from which the body had been removed, as though fearful that the spirit of the departed might return at any moment and resume command over his household.

Sylvester Drew cleared his throat with a nervous cough and addressed himself to the little group who sat forward in hushed anticipation.

"As executor of your late uncle's estate, I have summoned you here to carry out his instructions." He chose a letter from among the papers in his hand and turned once more to his little audience. "I am authorized to pay to his housekeeper the sum of five thousand dollars as her share of the estate for her loyal services during the past twenty years, with this one provision: that she continue to run the house for the next year in accordance with the desires set forth in the letter which I am about to read to you."

The housekeeper brushed a tear from her eye as she murmured a faint "God rest his soul." Drew helped himself to a glass of water, opened the letter in question and began:

"To my nephews: I chuckle as I think what consternation this message is likely to cause. I am getting along in years; this old heart of mine is none too strong, and the doctor tells me I am likely to pass out at any time . . . .

"I could leave my property to some worthy charity, but I hate the idea of letting it go out of the family. You three nephews none of whom I have ever seen, are my nearest living relatives. I suppose the right thing to do would be to divide it equally among you, but knowing as little about you as I do I hesitate to take this step. Instead, I have evolved this plan:

"I have placed several copies of instructions for the disposition of my property in conspicuous places about this big house of mine. I doubt if anyone would recognize them as such, however, without directions for finding them.

"I have made three copies of such directions, one for each of you, and have instructed my lawyer to see that a copy is placed in each of your hands. If, at the end of one year from my death, none of you has succeeded in interpreting them, the bulk of my estate goes to some worthy charity to be selected by the executor.

"The house will be kept open until the expiration of the time limit I have given you and, to those of you who wish to give all your time to the search for the missing instructions, an allowance will be granted to cover ordinary contingent expenses.

"As a greater part of my life has been given over to solving the problems of others, it affords me a great deal of pleasure to leave behind me a problem of my own for someone else to wrestle with. May the best man win!

"Just a word more, and I will bring this letter to a close. Some wise man has compared life to a game of cards, and pointed out that the winner is the one who holds the best hands. To me, however, Life---aye, and Death---is more like a gigantic game of solitaire, in which each one of us must play a lone hand.

Your uncle,

Josiah Keene."

The lawyer paused for breath and again pawed over the sheaf of letters. He separated three of them, and advanced upon the waiting trio.

"Mr. Newman . . . Mr. Fales . . . and Mr. Keene. Of course, gentlemen, you understand that it is not compulsory for you to enter upon this seemingly crazy quest; but unless you do, the bulk of the estate goes to some charity of my selection."

Three envelopes were opened almost simultaneously; three pairs of eyes scanned the enclosures with avid interest; three faces registered blank bewilderment as they gazed upon the unintelligible message before them:

"2D2CQD2H6S8C9SQCKH8D9D4H2C8S9S6CKC8D2H

7C2CQS2H8S7DQH2S7H9D7C2CQD2H8D4CKH2D10S7H."

Giles Newman was the first to recover from the initial shock of surprise. A brawny hand came down with a resounding whack upon a stocky thigh, and his big voice boomed out in ill-timed laughter.

"The joke's on me, alright, boys! Here I've traveled clean across the continent to see that old Uncle Joe gets a decent burial, and this is what I get handed to me! Well, I'm game to make a stab for the old miser's millions. Guess I've got as much of a chance as the next fellow. What's the dope, Drew, on this allowance business?"

The other nephews eyed Newman will ill-concealed displeasure. The housekeeper broke off her subdued sobbing to cast a wrathful glance at the speaker. Drew maintained a dignified silence as he consulted his documents for the required information.

"The conditions require, " he responded, "that the recipient of such an allowance shall reside in this house and take his meals here. A sum of fifty dollars should be placed at his disposal each week for incidental expenses. It is understood, of course, that this offer automatically expires if the secret is discovered by any one of the nephews prior to the explanation of the time limit."

Newman stuck two pudgy thumbs in the armholes of his vest, tilted back his chair, and announced in his bellowing tone:

"Suits me to a 'T'." He shot a questioning look at his cousins. "What d'y'say, boys? Goin' to give me a run for the money or let me have it all by my lonesome?"

The others exchanged glances. The lawyer tapped a

nervous tattoo with his fingers upon the arm of the chair. An awkward silence fell upon the little group, punctuated at length by Newman's impatient:

"Well?"

Harland Fales' sallow cheeks flushed slightly at the pertinent query. He drew his lanky figure more stiffly erect in his chair before he returned:

"It strikes me as being almost irreverent, so soon after our late uncle's burial, to plunge head long into a discussion of such a cold-blooded proposition as this one. Still, I suppose that it is necessary that we make our decisions as soon as possible. Cousin Giles is not the only one who has left home and business miles behind. I, too, feel that the stake is too big not to strive for, but I wish it could be arranged so that we would all have an equal opportunity. I, for one, must start for home tomorrow. Otherwise, should this quest prove futile, my business interests would suffer complete annihilation."

"Allow me to venture a suggestion." All eyes focused upon Roger Keene. "The element of chance seems to figure a great deal in this whole affair. Suppose we invoke the Goddess still further? There are three of us. Let us draw lots, each to spend four months here, in turn, to pursue our search. This will obviate the friction that would certainly occur should we all take up our residence here at the same time. If any of us should succeed in solving this cryptic message in the interim, he will of course be privileged to come here and continue his hunt for the missing instructions."

"An admirable suggestion." Lawyer Drew nodded sagely as he voiced his approval. Fales signaled silent acquiescence, while Newman's stentorian voice boomed forth once more.

"I'm game! I'm a sport, I am! Anything suits you, suits me. Make out your tickets and I'll show you how to pick a winner!"

His jocular mood, his flippant attitude, jarred visibly upon the nerves of the others. Again that awesome hush closed in about them.

The offender failed to sense it, however. After a moment's inaction he swung his ponderous frame to its full height, crossed to the table, ripped a few sheets from his note-book, scrawled a big number on each of them, and tossed them into a cut-glass dish he found there.

" 'Smatter with you fellows? You act like you was doped or something! Here!" He strode back across the room and halted before the pale-faced Fales. "Stick you mitt in there, and' see what luck you have!"

Harland Fales complied. His fingers trembled slightly as he unfolded the slip of paper he had drawn. A sigh of relief escaped him as he looked upon the big figure three scrawled there.

Giles passed the dish to his remaining cousin. "Try your luck, Roger," he taunted.

Calmly, without a sign of undue haste, Roger Keene selected the slip which assigned him to the second third of the year. Newman confiscated the remaining paper with a hoarse chuckle.

"There's your Uncle Dudley's meal ticket for a while, boys," he grinned. "You might's well quit before you start. While you unlucky boobs are puzzlin' your brains tryin' t' dope out that Chinese puzzle, I'll be scoutin' around here after them missin' papers. An' I'll find 'em, or my name aint Giles Newman! Even if I have t' wreck the whole sheebang!"

Sylvester Drew rose.

"I think I must be getting back to the office," he told them. "If there is anything about this that you don't understand, feel free to call upon me at any time within the year. And you may find, gentlemen," the corners of his mouth curved slightly in a quizzical smile, "that a year, long as it may seem, may prove all too short to complete your task. Your late uncle, as you are all aware, was rated one of the foremost cryptographers the country has ever known! I assure you it will be no child's play. Good afternoon---and good luck to all of you!"

* * * * * * *

Roger Keene had scarcely touched foot to the station platform when a brawny hand shot out to meet his own and a voice, familiar despite the lapse of time, boomed into his ear:

"Got your wire, Old Timer. Felt 'twas up t' me t' do the honors. Gimme that grip of yours an' hop into the flivver. We'll be up home in two shakes of a lamb's tail!"

Giles Newman guffawed boisterously at his cousin's confusion as he piloted Keene to a seat in the machine and tossed the suitcase carelessly into the rear. A moment later they were on the road.

"Bought it with what I saved out of the old man's fifty a week," he confided. "She's cheap, but she covers the ground!" His face lost a bit of its habitual cheerfulness. "Guess it's all I'll have to show for my four months' vacation. I've ransacked that old rat-trap from garret to cellar. You've got it all doped out, I s'pose? "

Keene shook his head.

"Not yet. Naturally, though, I have hopes. I've put in every bit of spare time on that cipher, but I'm still up against a stone wall."

"H-huh?" Giles swung the car to the left to pass a loaded hay-wagon. "Better wish on that. Maybe it'll bring you luck!"

"Thanks. The same to you. You have the rest of the year, you know."

"Not me! I'm done! Four months in this burg is enough for yours truly! I'm leaving bright an' early in the morning. You won't be lonesome, though. Fales is in town."

"Fales?" Roger Keene's brow clouded.

"Uh-huh! Got in on the noon train. Called up from Drew's office and said he'd be up for supper. Reg'lar family party, eh?"

The cousins lapsed into sudden taciturnity which they maintained during the rest of the ride over the rutted road. Keene had scarcely finished unpacking his things when Fales and Drew arrived in the lawyer's car. The lawyer refused an invitation to stay for the evening meal, and his car chugged away in the growing dusk, leaving the cousins alone.

Supper was hardly a success. The housekeeper's most choice morsels went begging. Even Giles Newman's attempted levity failed to dispel the veiled enmity among the trio.

But it was not until he lighted his cigar, that Harland Fales confirmed their suspicions. His sallow face was flushed with excitement and enthusiasm.

"I'm honestly sorry boys. You've had all your work for nothing, but I 'm on the right trail to Uncle Josiah's millions, and if all goes well, the mystery will be solved before morning.

"I wanted to be sure I was within my rights to come here before you, Roger, had stayed out your time, so I went straight to Drew's office when I got into town.

"He pointed out that this matter of four months apiece was merely an arbitrary arrangement among ourselves, and that according to Uncle Josiah's instructions, any one of us was entitled to the freedom of the house at any time within the year.

"So here I am! Now, if you'll excuse me, I'll retire to the library and get to work. If I'm on the right track, I'll be through before morning. If not, I'll pack up and go when you do, Giles, so that Roger may have a free hand."

Newman and Keene spent the long evening in earnest discussion. It was eleven when the pair rapped on the library door and called good-night to Fales.

"I'd ask you in, boys," came back his voice, "but the way things are breaking, it might tip you off to the secret of the cryptogram. See you in the morning, and tell you the answer. 'Night!"

By midnight the big house was silent as a tomb. Only the light gleaming from the library window would have given a clue to the chance passer-by of the man who worked with feverish intensity to accomplish his mission.

Both Roger Keene and his cousin were up with the sun, but Harland Fales failed to put in an appearance at the breakfast table.

"Don't know's I blame him much," rumbled Giles " 'Specially if that hunch of his was a bloomer! He prob'ly set up half the night, provin' himself wrong!" He tipped the bowl to scoop out the last spoonful of oatmeal but stopped, suddenly, at the terrified scream that rang through the old mansion.

As one, the cousins raced for the hall in the direction of the sound, almost stumbling over the body of the old housekeeper who lay huddled before the partly opened library door.

"Get some water, Giles," commanded Keene. "You know the layout of the house better than I do. I'll see what's wrong." He turned from the senseless woman and pushed wide the library door. With an effort, he repressed a cry of terror.

In the center of the room, directly in his line of vision, was a massive, flattop desk. A large, roomy arm chair was drawn up before it, and it was upon this that Roger Keene's attention was centered. Slumped forward in the chair, chin sagging upon his breast, head crushed in like an egg-shell, eyes wide and staring, was the body of Harland Fales!

Keene swept the room in an all-encompassing glance. No trace of a weapon was visible. At the left, the wall was lined with bookcases. At the right, a full-length oil painting of his Uncle Josiah looked down upon the scene of tragedy with calm, complacent eyes. Directly below this, stood an old-fashioned Bible stand, and upon it one of those now out of date family Bibles, more unwieldly than an unabridged dictionary---the kind which used to grace every Christian home.

"Keene's gaze returned to the man in the chair. Overcoming his natural repugnance, he advanced towards the gruesome discovery. As he neared the body, he noticed something which had escaped him at first. In the hand which dangled lifelessly over the chair arm, Fales tightly clutched two playing cards. Others were scattered about upon the floor between the chair and the desk, where they were invisible from the door. The remainder of the pack was laid out in orderly fashion atop the desk.

A single glance sufficed to tell that Harland Fales had met his death while playing solitaire. He noted, too, that the long French window at the far end of the room was open wide.

By this time Newman had returned and the pair gave their attention to the housekeeper. After they had restored the woman to some semblance of composure, Keene queried:

"Now, Mrs. Baxter, whatever has happened?"

"I don't know, sir. I thought I'd set things to rights a bit, while you were having breakfast. I opened the library door, and----" she broke off, and her frame trembled, "Well, that's all I remember, 'till I opened my eyes and found you here."

"Better go up and lie down," Newman urged. Then, to Keene. "We'd better get Drew, right away."

They watched her out of sight up the winding stairway. Then, rapidly thumbing the pages of the telephone book, Newman notified the lawyer and the authorities.

Coroner Draper, Inspector Little and Sylvester Drew arrived within a few moments of one another.

John Draper, was the typical country practitioner. Of medium build, with mild blue eyes and a quiet manner, he made a hasty, albeit complete examination of the body. Keene set him down as one who, while an efficient physician, had obtained his post as coroner through sheer political pull.

While he was engaged in making his examination, Keene tried to size up his companion.

Inspector Little belonged to the vast army of inaptly named individuals we meet from day to day. A ponderous frame, six-foot-two of well set up manhood, a large head and a bull-dog jaw. The fringe of hair that formed a half-circle around his bald pate was tinged with gray, a match for his steely, gimlet eyes.

The coroner, his examination completed, turned back to the anxious group with a solemn nod.

"Looks bad, Little. The fact that the weapon is missing would in itself, be suspicious, but the position of the body and the crushed condition of the skull preclude any possibility of accidental injury."

The inspector returned his nod.

"How long's he been dead, Doc?"

"As near as I can determine, since about two this morning."

"Um-m-m." Little turned to the cousins. "Who discovered him?"

"Mrs. Baxter, the housekeeper." Keene told of her scream and the subsequent discoveries. Newman corroborated him.

"It's a damn shame!" Newman exploded at the conclusion of his testimony. My four months are up, an' I was planning' to get out of this burg, today!"

"Four months up? What do you mean?"

"Why, y'see, Inspector---"

Sylvester Drew stepped forward.

"If you'll pardon me, Inspector," he interpolated, I'll

try to explain. My client, the late Mr. Keene, left rather a peculiar will." Little nodded for him to continue and the lawyer went on, laying particular stress on the drawing of lots by the cousins and on the advice he had given Fales the afternoon before.

Then Little questioned them as to their movements on the preceding evening.

"Let me see now," he summarized, "You both sat talkin' until about eleven. Then you both went upstairs to your rooms, biddin' good-night to your cousin on the way. That's O.K., seein' as the Doc says he wasn't killed until nearly two.

"You, Keene, say you went right to bed. And you, Newman, claim you packed your suitcase, then did likewise. A fine pair of alibis!

"How do we know you did? How do we know what you were talkin' about while your cousin was shut up in the library? How do we know but what one---maybe both---of you, sneaked out about two o'clock, tiptoed in through the French window, there, and slammed him over the skull while he was too busy workin' out the puzzle to hear you comin'?

"If you want my honest opinion, I think one of you is lyin'! Maybe both! Damfino-yet!" He turned to the coroner.

"Here's the way I figure it, Doc. One of these guys, or maybe both, as I said before, figured if this chap did have the right dope on that cipher, all chance for the old man's money was gone. It all fits in---motive, opportunity, and all! "

"Now, Inspector!" Draper's tone was placating. "Don't you think you've said more than enough until you make sure of your ground?"

"Maybe you're right Doc. I don't want to show my hand too soon. But so am I right about one of these birds bein' guilty! And I'll get the goods on him, too, before I'm many days older. Come on, Draper, let's go!"

After promising to make arrangements for the disposition of the body, Sylvester Drew followed them.

* * * * * * *

A week passed swiftly. Inspector Little had spent hours in the big house, and had grilled the cousins mercilessly, but matters were at a standstill.

No clues had been unearthed, nor a single trace found of the elusive weapon. Little, despite his boasts and threats, had proved nothing.

In his own mind, much as he hated to admit it, Roger Keene was beginning to agree with the Inspector that one of the two cousins was guilty---and that it was Giles Newman!

For the first time since his cousin's body had been removed, Keene pushed open the door of the library. Already a light layer of dust had settled upon the furnishings. Mrs. Baxter had flatly refused to make any attempt to straighten things out, and Roger felt it was up to him to tidy up a bit.

He crossed to the desk in the center of the room. The cards were still laid out in orderly fashion on its top. Someone, probably the inspector, had picked up the few that had been strewn about on the floor, and tossed them into the arm chair. Keene rescued these, and dropped into their place. He could scarcely repress a slight shudder as he remembered that this was the chair in which the dead man had been discovered.

His eyes dropped to the cards upon the desk.

Solitaire! Somehow, the word recalled the group that had met in his late uncle's parlor the afternoon following the funeral. For a moment, he failed to grasp the connection. Then he remembered. It was something his uncle had written, near the close of the letter the lawyer had read to them. What was it now? Oh, yes, he knew!

". . . Life---aye, and Death---is more like a gigantic game of solitaire, in which each one of us must play a lone hand!"

And his cousin, Harland Fales, had come to his death while playing solitaire. He wondered if it could be a mere coincidence.

He fell to riffling the loose cards between his fingers. They were old and dog-eared. He wondered, too, if they were Fales', or if they had belonged to his Uncle Josiah. He looked at them more closely.

All at once he came bolt upright in his chair. Just below the tiny figure in the upper, right hand corner of the six of spades was scrawled, in an almost obliterated pencil mark, a different letter!

In eager haste he began his arrangement of the cards upon the desk. His cheeks were flushed with excitement, and his hands shook slightly. If he was right, the wealth of old Josiah Keene lay within his grasp.

At last the entire pack lay out before him, in two long rows. For each letter of the alphabet, he found two cards. He noticed that the suits alternated, always in the same order---clubs, diamonds, hearts and spades .

In feverish haste he took pencil and paper, and lined up the following key to the mysterious cipher message:

A B C D E F G H I J K L M N O P Q R S T U V W X Y Z
8 K 3 10 2 7 9 5 Q 4 1 6 J 8 K 3 10 2 7 9 5 Q 4 1 6 J
C D H S C D H S C D H S C D H S C D H S C D H S C D
H S C D H S C D H S C D H S C D H S C D H S C D H S

He ransacked his pockets for a copy of the cryptogram. At last he remembered that it was in his bedroom. Enroute to the stairs, the phone caught his eye, and he paused long enough to get Drew on the wire and tell him that he held the solution of the mystery in the hollow of his hand. Drew agreed to come out to the old house at once, and learn the answer to the riddle.

It may have been purely his imagination, but Keene could have sworn he saw Giles Newman disappear into the parlor as he turned away from the phone. Had he been eavesdropping? If so, how much had he overheard? By the time he reached the door of the parlor the room was empty.

Again at the desk in the library, Roger Keene spread the code message before him with nerveless fingers. One by one he deciphered the letters of the communication, until at last the secret was before his eyes.

REVELATION TWENTY ONE SEVEN FIRST SEVEN WORDS

He paused in blank astonishment. Was this but another cryptic message? Would it prove to be a double cipher, after all?

He seemed to feel eyes looking piercingly upon him. He turned to stare at the oil painting of his late uncle. His eyes dropped to the big family Bible on the stand below.

In a flash he understood. *Revelation!* Could any more fitting place be found for a solution of the riddle? He opened the unwieldy volume to the last book of the New Testament. He turned the pages to the twenty-first chapter, then followed down the column until his finger stopped at the seventh verse.

The first seven words:

"He that overcometh shall inherit all things. . . ."

The book was heavy. Keene followed the line of least resistance, and closed it, face downward, upon the stand. Subconsciously, he noted something odd about it. He looked closer. His face paled with a new horror.

Revelation!

In more ways than one was this book destined to solve the riddles of the mystic maze which engulfed him! The back cover of the Bible was splotched with dried, red stains. Here was the weapon which had crushed the skull of his cousin, Harland Fales!

There was a sudden, sharp crash of breaking glass; the report of an unseen revolver, and Roger Keene crumpled in an inert heap to the floor.

* * * * * * *

When he opened his eyes, Keene was lying on the big lounge in the old-fashioned parlor, while the housekeeper was adjusting a bandage about his head.

He looked around him. He was sure he must be dreaming it all. First, Newman's big bulk caught his eye. Beyond him was the towering figure of Inspector Little. But most surprising of all, was the portly form of Sylvester Drew, manacled firmly to the detective.

Giles Newman was upon him in a trice, pumping his arm, while his big voice boomed out like a fog horn.

"Nothin' but a scratch, Roger, old man. We'll have you 'round again in a shake of a cow's tail!"

Little refused to be denied his say.

"Better thank your cousin, Keene, that old Doc Draper won't have the pleasure of holdin' another inquest." He jerked savagely at the handcuffs which fastened the lawyer's wrist to his own. "This guy, here, seems to have a mania for killin' off the Keene family, in all its branches. Suppose you tell him what you told me, Newman, while I pack this shyster where he won't play with pop-guns or smash any more skulls for awhile."

"I sized up Drew for the killer soon's I had a chance to think straight," Newman explained, after Little had left with his prisoner, "But that doggone copper was ridin' us so hard I didn't dare say anything 'till I had the goods on him! With his knowledge of the house an' grounds, he'd have as much chance as we did. As for motive, if none of us solved the puzzle, the property would pass into his hands. Fat chance any charity would have had, gettin' any of it.

"I heard you phone him this afternoon an' I kept my eyes open. I was layin' for him, outside. Instead of rappin' at the door, he sneaked 'round the veranda to the French window and picked you off.

"I guess he must have gone plumb loco when he saw you foolin' 'round that Bible. Otherwise, he'd never have risked shootin' through the glass, like he did, in broad daylight. Maybe he figured his only chance was to put you out of the running an' framin' things so's I'd have to stand the gaff.

"He'd have got away with it, too, if he hadn't been a

little slow on the draw. I jogged his arm just in time. I hog-tied him an' phoned the inspector. Little says his fingerprints are all over the back cover of the Bible."

Roger Keene nodded.

"It was clever at that, Giles. There wasn't but one chance in a million that any one of us would touch that old Bible. Talk about overlooking the obvious! But then, who'd ever think of using a Bible to kill a man!"

Newman yawned. "So that's that! Both mysteries solved at once. Now little Giles can trot home happy. An', Roger," half-whimsically, "this ain't such a dead burg, after all."

A few hours later the cousins stood beneath the portrait of their late uncle, above the now empty Bible stand. Newman grasped his cousin's hand.

"Congratulations, Old Timer! You brought home the bacon, after all."

Roger Keene shook his head and turned his eyes to the picture on the wall.

"Uncle Josiah says 'No,' Giles. If it hadn't been for you, my work on the cipher would have done me as little good as Fales'. I refuse to play solitaire any more, Giles . . . even in sharing rewards!"

Black Noon

EVEN AS FAR BACK as the late '20s I was already an inveterate reader. There seemed to be something special I gained from settling back in my armchair after a hard day's work, with a fresh stock of fiction magazines and my favorite pipe, and completely losing myself in the synthetic adventures spun by the most popular writers of the era.

Nobody knew that any better than old Pop Ferguson, who ran the Fenham News Depot. I think I was his biggest single buyer of the scores of publications that flooded the stands. But that did not mean that every time I went into the store I was on the prowl for reading matter. In fact, on this particular afternoon I had stopped in to pick up a pouch of pipe tobacco to accompany the arm-load of magazines I had carted home only the day before.

"Hi, ya, Biff," Pop greeted me, "Got a minute to spare? A brand new one showed up, today. Thought you might like a look-see, so I tucked it under the counter 'til you came in. I'll get it for you, right away. "

Pop sure had my number. I waited; it seemed no time at all before I was holding in my hands a copy of the newest attempt to catch a reader's eyes, with one of the most flamboyant covers I'd seen in years. Across the top was emblazoned in inch-high letters its title: "Uncanny Stories." And, though it was only the tenth of August, away over near the right hand edge of the cover, it was dated "September, 1927."

"It's a first issue, Biff," Pop started his sales talk. "Volume one, number one. Might be worth a lot of money one of these days."

"Twenty-five cents," I whistled, softly. Most of the fiction magazines in those days were priced at a dime, or at the most fifteen cents. However, I'd told him I'd take it, so I paid him for it and my tobacco, and headed home with my newest acquisition to contemporary literature under my arm with the firm intention of trying to get my quarter's worth out of it right after supper.

You know the old saying about the best laid plans. Right after eating, the phone kept me tied up for a couple of hours. That's one of the penalties of running one's own business. When jobs are coming in, you just can't afford to let personal pleasure interfere. By the time the calls had ceased, and I'd laid out at least a tentative schedule that would keep all my customers satisfied, there was only enough reading time left for me to catch up on the installments of a couple of serials I was following in the periodicals I'd purchased the night before.

But the next night was free from such interruptions, and I was soon entrenched for the evening, pipe alight, and an attitude that challenged "Uncanny Stories" to thrill me.

I noticed a line at the bottom of the cover which had

escaped my attention in the store: "All stories complete in this issue," and I wondered how they expected to hold reader interest from one month to another. With a shrug I opened to the contents page and scanned it rapidly. Despite all the reading I'd done over the years, not a single author's name was familiar. So much for that. I turned to the first story with the intention of reading it right through from cover to cover.

The yarns contained all the stock ingredients that are considered the requisites of this type of tale,---the haunted house with its thunderstorm and ghosts with clanking chains, the fog-enshrouded graveyard with its ghouls; werewolves, vampires, voodooism and all the rest. But something was lacking. Most of them were so utterly fantastic as to be completely unbelievable. They left me cold. Maybe I wasn't in the right mood. By the time I'd waded halfway through the issue I was heartily disgusted and about ready to toss the book aside, but I'm a stubborn sort of guy, and after all I had an investment of two-bits in the darn thing, and I still hoped to get my money's worth. A glance at the clock, and I decided to read one more story before calling it quits.

With all the years of reading behind me, I pride myself that I can recognize top-notch writing the minute I come across it. In fact, if I could pick horses as accurately as I can name potential winners in the writing game, I'd be a millionaire. Maybe I missed my calling and should have been a magazine editor !

I knew after the first couple of pages that here was a story that would appeal to the more intelligent readers of the magazine. It was slower-paced than the previous yarns, noticeably so after the slam-bang style in which the others had been told; you could almost call it leisurely, yet I had the feeling as I read that it was not padded, that every carefully chosen word was advancing the reader to a terrifying climax. The author hinted at hidden horrors so terrible as to be beyond mere words to depict, at malignant entities too blasphemous to be grasped by mortal mind, evil putrescences who had lurked for untold eons in the vast void beyond human knowledge, waiting for the rare opportunity to break through the barriers and wreak havoc upon some supersensitive human being and grasp him up into their rapacious maw. Every phrase, every sentence, every paragraph built up the tension, the suspense, and by the time I reached the denouement, little icicles were playing hopscotch up and down my spine and I could feel the cold sweat on my brow.

I sank back in my chair and mopped the moisture from my forehead. The impact of the story had left me breathless, emotionally exhausted. That writer was great! I suddenly remembered I hadn't even noticed his name. I rapidly ran through the pages of the magazine to the beginning of the masterpiece. There it was, both title and author:

EXIT
By Robert Otis Mather

And I let my mind go back to see if I could remember ever having seen the name before. No luck. I was about to toss the issue aside, when a sudden impulse moved me to flip over the pages in search of something. I finally found it. The usual appeal on the part of the editor of a new publication urging the readers to write in and express their opinions. For the first---and only---time in my life I did that very thing. In my frame of mind I said some rather unkind things about the magazine as a whole, but I went all out in my praise of "Exit" and its author, Robert Otis Mather. I sealed and stamped the letter so that it would be ready to drop in the post office on my way to work in the morning, made a mental note to tell Pop Ferguson to save me the next couple of issues, shook out my pipe and headed for bed.

September tenth arrived before I realized it, and with it came the second issue of "Uncanny Stories." I looked over the new letters from readers section which consisted of two pages of wishes for success from well-known authors in all branches of the fiction field, scanned the contents, decided that none of the stories justified wasting my time reading them, and tossed it on my evergrowing pile of magazines.

But the tenth of October held two things of interest for me. My letter turned up in the November number, the only one that even mentioned Mather's story---and the editor's note that he agreed with my appraisal of "Exit" to such a degree that he had already purchased two more by the same author, the first of which would appear in the next month's issue. It gave me sort of a letdown feeling when I picked up the December "Uncanny" and failed to find Mather's name on the cover. It was listed on the contents page, however, immediately following the featured novelette. This time it was a story of Salem in the days of the witchcraft purge, told with the same master craftmanship, the same wizardry of words that enthralled me to the very last paragraph.

Then I was plunged headlong into the holiday activities that engulf most towns, large or small. The Armistice Day parade with the clean-up job that always followed in its wake, decorating the town for Thanksgiving, the start of plans for the Christmas season. The first, light November snowfall, with the residents sweeping sidewalks frantically to get them spotlessly clean before the sudden drop in temperature that always followed. Overcoats, scarves and gloves to combat those first few really cold fall days. My reading was always side-tracked for a few weeks every year until things settled back to a normal routine, so that I was totally unprepared for the telephone call when it came.

I was barely inside the house after an early evening business call which resulted in an attractive contract, when the phone rang. I tossed my hat in the chair and picked up the receiver. An attractive, well-modulated feminine voice answered my opening greeting.

"Mr. Briggs?" I signified my assent, and the voice continued, "If you are not too busy, Mr. Mather would like to speak to you."

"Mr. Who?"

"Mr. Mather, Mr. Robert Otis Mather. Just hold the line, please."

I could scarcely believe my ears! If this was who I thought it was, why in the world would he be calling me? And where was he calling from? At that moment, a new voice reached my ear.

"I asked my aunt to establish telephonic contact for me, because such modern mechanical contrivances find little favor in my eyes, and I only use it when I find it more expedient than less rapid forms of communication. The editor of 'Uncanny Stories' forwarded your fan note to me. He thought I might be interested to note that we both reside in the same town. I was, indeed, so interested that I called to ask if your interest in my work could be extended to dropping in for a visit some evening soon, so that we might become better acquainted."

For a moment I was speechless. The silence was broken by his voice inquiring:

"Mr. Briggs, are you still there?"

I was, and I told him so.

"You probably know where Spring Lane is located, at the east end of the town? I live at number thirty-one. I'm here every evening at this time of the year. How about some night early next week, say about eight-thirty?"

I recovered sufficiently to accept his invitation for the following Tuesday. After assuring me he would be looking forward to the occasion with keen anticipation, he said his good-byes and the phone went dead.

Of course I knew where Spring Lane was. The east end of Fenham was sharply divided into two major sections---the newly developed area with its more modern mansions where our local ultra-ultra set was domiciled, and the older part of the town, just beyond it, with its fast disappearing Colonial dwellings that dated back to the earlier days of Fenham, which housed what we were pleased to class as our respectable gentility---those quiet souls who main desire seemed to be keeping up with the Joneses. Spring Lane was in the latter group, and I hardly knew anyone by name in that end of town. Yet it seemed improbable to me that a man such as Robert Otis Mather could become absorbed in the life of our community without even a mention of his name in our local weekly, but the only time I had ever come across it was in the magazine to which he was now a contributor.

The next few days seemed to drag. I began to feel the same combination of exhilaration and impatience I had experienced when, as a boy, my Dad had promised to take me to the circus for the first time.

Tuesday night turned out to be a beautiful one, weatherwise. One of those crisp, cold, clear late November evenings before the heavy storm of the winter struck our section of New England. I honestly enjoyed the brisk, mile walk from where I lived to the east end, and halted outside the three-foot hedge that enclosed 31 Spring Lane. I hesitated a moment before advancing up the ancient flagstoned pathway. I noticed a light through the fan-shaped windows that formed an arc above the front door, raised the old-fashioned knocker and rapped, not too sharply.

"Good-evening, Mr. Briggs," I recognized the same voice I had heard over the telephone, "I'm Agatha Sessions, Robert's aunt. Just hang your wraps on the rack and come right into the living room." I followed her inside, where she indicated a comfortable chair, and continued, "I hope you don't mind waiting a few moments. Robert is just finishing his breakfast."

Breakfast? At eight-thirty in the evening?

The aunt answered my unspoken questions.

"Robert's pattern for living is essentially nocturnal, as you'll realize if you get to know him better. The night is his working day. Another thing is his allergy to winter weather.

The cold actually makes him physically ill. As a result he practically hibernates from early fall to late spring." She arose as a bell tinkled from the adjoining room. "That's Robert now. He's in his den and will be ready to see you as soon as I remove his dishes." She emerged from the room, tray in hand, and called to me. "All right, Mr. Briggs, you can go in any time, now."

I don't know what I expected my first glimpse of Robert Otis Mather to be like, but any preconceived notions I may have had were a long way from reality.

The den was a reasonably large room, lined on three sides from floor to ceiling with shelves that were filled with books, books, and still more books---books as I found out later which ranged through almost every known category. In one corner of the room was a small, castered table on which rested what looked at first glance to be one of the oldest models of typewriters made. In another corner was a neatly-stacked, double pile of newspapers. Centered along the remaining wall was a massive, utilitarian table, flanked on either side by more books. The table was piled high with letters, manuscripts and writing materials. At the end of the table nearest the door was a comfortable-looking vacant chair. At the only other chair in the room, near the center of the long table, was the man I had come to see.

"Good-evening, Mr. Briggs," he greeted me, as I crossed the room towards where he was sitting and, without rising, stretched a long arm in my direction. At a quick glance I took in his jet-black hair, the large, round, smiling black eyes, his high cheek-bones and the hollows beneath them. I was a bit surprised at the firmness of his grip when we

"Pardon me for not getting up to welcome you, but I just didn't have the heart to disturb Blossom."

I followed his eyes to his lap, and there, completely relaxed and apparently asleep, was the largest calico cat I think I had ever seen. So that was Blossom! She must have weighed at least twenty pounds! Her body sagged slightly in the space between his knees, where he had spread them to keep the cat's huge bulk from overhanging at the limits of his lap.

"Cats have always had a special appeal for me. I like them much better than dogs," Mather was saying as I took my place in the vacant chair. "I think it's their independence I admire. A dog can, and often does, become an abject slave to its master, but a cat confers its favors on we humans only when and if she so desires. But I'm quite sure, Mr. Briggs, you didn't come all the way across town primarily to discuss cats. Probably there are subjects of more importance on your agenda."

"Frankly, Mr. Mather, I think it was a two-fold curiosity that prompted my visit. In the first place, with all my years of being a rabid fiction fan, I had never met a real live author, and being a native of Fenham I felt I had missed out somewhere along the line in not knowing we harbored one in our midst."

Mather chuckled. At first sound of my voice, Blossom lazily opened one eye and studied me for a moment, rose, stretched, eased herself from his lap and ambled across the den to the double pile of newspapers, leaped lightly atop them with a grace and agility that belied her weight and size, and curled up to resume her interrupted siesta.

"Blossom isn't used to strangers," he explained. "In fact, it is the first time since she adopted us a little over two years ago that a guest has invaded our sanctum of sanctums." He gestured toward the stack of mail on his work table. "Despite my voluminous correspondence across America and Canada I don't think I've met more than a dozen of my pen pals in person."

He reached toward a pile of manuscripts, lifted off the topmost one and handed it to me.

"My last effort to keep the editor of 'Uncanny' happy. He's been after me for the last two weeks for another story. Just completed it last night and haven't yet had a chance to give it a final going over before Agatha types it. My aunt has been a tremendous help to me. Before I'd venture to wrestle with that mechanical metal monster in the corner I'd prefer never to sell a word."

I glanced at the script. What a mess. Every page had been practically rewritten, with the spaces between the lines and the margins almost completely filled. To read it would be like trying to solve a Chinese puzzle. Mather sensed my dilemma, and took back the story with a smile.

"I'd forgotten for the moment how difficult folks find it to decipher my chirography. Suppose I read it aloud, Mr. Briggs, if you don't think it would bore you to tears."

I had already found out from the reading that Robert Otis Mather was a top-notch writer. He now proved himself an equally proficient reader with a Thespian flair for vocal impressions of his characters that lent verity to the word pictures he had painted. The setting was one of Colonial days, and while he was reading I felt that I had been transported back to those days and could visualize the scenes as he described them. The story built up masterfully to its horror-filled culmination, and left me with all the makings of a night of emotionally induced hag-ridden dreams.

I said as much to Mather after I regained my composure, and took the liberty to add:

"I don't see how you can continually write that sort of stuff without being affected by it, yet you seem as cool and calm as if you'd been reading a page or two of history."

"Mr. Briggs, I haven't the slightest belief in any of that sort of supernatural twaddle. In fact, I think I'm safe in saying there isn't one dram of superstition in my entire makeup. These things I try to write about are purely figments of imagination, with a foundation laid only in ancient legend, folklore, or old wive's tales, born and bred in ignorance and nurtured by the stubborness of those who believe to admit the blazing light of science and education into their bigoted minds!"

I don't know when I had more thoroughly enjoyed an evening, but after a few minutes of small talk, and faced with the necessity of a mile walk home and a job to go to in the morning, I accepted with alacrity his invitation to repeat the visit the following Tuesday evening, and rose to take my leave. I was surprised when Blossom left her pile of papers and came over to rub against my ankles, purr loudly, and condescend to allow me to pat her good-night.

The next few weeks were some of the happiest I had ever spent in my life. Tuesday became my regular night to turn up at 31 Spring Lane. One of the things I enjoyed most was the element of never knowing what facet of Mather's many-sided literary personality would be displayed when I arrived.

For instance, my second trip found him hard at work on the third in a series of four articles on astronomy that Robert was doing for a national publication. This one explained where the stars and constellations would appear in the sky during the fall of 1928. The diagrams and maps which he was drawing to send along with the story showed a grasp of celestial cartography unexcelled in its accuracy.

On my next visit he was in the midst of ghost-writing a group of short lectures on psychology for a noted speaker who needed some new material for his annual Spring tour. And the next week he was trying to get caught up with some of his correspondence, which consisted mostly of stories and poems from amateur writers who sought his advice and revision on their efforts.

I certainly would have missed those Tuesday evenings had anything interfered. I not only got pleasure and satisfaction from our weekly gab fest, but I felt that if I continued to expose myself to so much talent and education that sooner or later a little of it might rub off on me.

By this time we'd reached a stage of informality where Robert was calling me "Biff," he was "Rom," the way he signed all his personal mail, and Miss Agatha Sessions was now "Aunt Aggie" to both of us.

It was just after the first of March that I noticed anything. Or, to be strictly truthful, that Blossom noticed it. I've often heard that cats are many times more psychic than humans. And I noticed Blossom. I couldn't put my finger on anything in particular, but I got the distinct impression that the Mather household was being invaded by an unseen presence that boded evil for all concerned. And, from the cat's actions, she and I agreed. Instead of her normal, phlegmatic self she was restless and uneasy. She would stop stock still in the room and stare intently in all four directions in turn as if she were trying to see the invisible force that disturbed her. Or she would sniff all around the room in and effort to make sense of smell locate that which she was unable to find visually. And twice during that same evening, once while sleeping on Rom's lap, and later when curled up comfortably atop the pile of papers, she leaped up suddenly as though from a nightmare, her back stiffened, her tail swished vigorously, and she was on the prowl around the den once more. I mentioned it to Rom, but he dismissed it briefly as an attack of indigestion. I shrugged my shoulders and dropped the subject.

My next evidence that something might be amiss was when, on my arrival a couple of weeks later, Aunt Aggie took time out to talk to me briefly before ushering me into the den.

"I don't know what is changing Robert," she began without preamble, "but the last few days I can't understand what has come over him. For the ten years he's been living with me, he's observed a set routine. Breakfast about eight in the evening, a snack around eleven, just before I went to bed, and his main meal when I was having my morning one. Then we'd chat while I helped him type his work of the night before, after which he'd retire and I'd go about my own daily tasks. Suddenly it's all changed. He's working all kinds of hours, he refuses the meals I prepare and is practically living on a diet of cheese, crackers, milk chocolate and tea. Frankly,

Biff, I'm worried about him!"

"I wouldn't get too fussed up about it if I were you, Aggie," I reassured her. "Not yet, at any rate. Whatever it is it will probably pass any time now, and he'll get back to the old routine." But I could see from the worry lines in her face that she was far from convinced.

"I hope you're right, Biff! Better go in now; he's expecting you."

As I neared the den I seemed to hear an unfamiliar clicking sound, but I never would have guessed its source until I saw for myself what had happened. The typewriter, table and all, had been moved out into the room adjacent to the work area and there was Robert Otis Mather sitting behind it, his fingers racing at top speed over the keyboard! I couldn't refrain from expressing my surprise.

"What's all this, Rom? Thought you couldn't type."

"Not couldn't Just didn't want to. But this is different. I've started the most important job in my writing career. I just can't leave it to anyone else. Not even Aggie." He spoke without even slowing down, indicated a stack of neatly typed pages with a nod, and continued. "I predict it will be my masterpiece,---a weird, fantastic trilogy---three complete novels about successive generations of the same family and the horrendous fate that pursued them through the years until it finally catches up with and eliminates the last of the line. Look some of it over, if you'd like. I need an outside opinion on what I've done so far." And still the unbroken sound of the typewriter continued.

I picked up the completed pages, and started to read. They gripped me from the very first paragraph. But before I was too far into the manuscript, I noticed two outstanding differences from his previous offerings. In the first place, the other stories of his that I had seen were laboriously penned by hand, then revised and rewritten page by page until he felt absolutely sure no further improvement could be made. These sheets were apparently just as they had come out of the machine, yet they needed no changes to bring them up to his usual high standards. It was uncanny, in a way, as though some higher intelligence had broken through the unbridgeable barrier between its mind and his and was dictating the story to him as rapidly as it could be transcribed and at the same time guiding his fingers over the ancient keyboard with a speed and accuracy that seemed utterly impossible. The other difference was in the tenor of the tale. This one was impregnated with a feeling of gruesomeness, malevolence and sadistic glee on the part of the demoniac dispensers of doom that had been conspicuously absent in the earlier tales.

The cat came into the room, circled it cautiously, and then instead of taking her usual place in Rom's lap, she jumped into mine, turned around three times and settled down for the evening. But not to sleep. Her eyes became mere slits through which she surveyed the room, turning her head slightly from time to time. She was alert, tense, ready for action. I stroked her fur and baby-talked her in an effort to relax her, but I couldn't get a single purr out of her. Her nervousness finally transmitted itself to me, and I found myself stealing surreptitious glances about the room, though for the life of me I couldn't have told anyone what I was looking for if anyone had asked me.

Were you ever in a room where two radios were going at the same time, each tuned to a different station? I got the same jumbled up effect sitting there listening to Rom talking a steady stream about every subject under the sun while all the time his fingers were beating an incessant tattoo on the keys, and he was grinding out page after page of a manuscript which to my mind should have required the utmost in undivided concentration. It was eerie, unnatural! It was just as though Robert's mind had been split into two separate and distinct sections, each working independently of the other, yet each fully cognizant of what the other half was doing. It gave me the creeps!

All through March the terrific pace continued. Aggie was becoming more worried as the days went on, the cat more upset and jittery, and I felt more out of place each time I called and watched that incessant type, type, typing. In fact, I think I might have cut out my weekly visits if I hadn't felt that my once a week chats with Aunt Aggie helped to bolster up her morale.

Then two things happened simultaneously. Rom wrote "finis" to his first novel---over one-hundred thousand words in a little over five weeks---perfect writing and typing that required only the slightest correction of typographical errors. And Aggie announced that Blossom had disappeared !

"Every morning I let the cat out after her breakfast and she goes for a stroll around the back yards of the neighborhood," Aggie explained. "Day before yesterday I let her out as usual, and we haven't seen her since. I spent all day today going from house to house and asking everybody, but nobody seems to have seen hide nor hair of her!"

"Stop worrying. She's probably locked up in somebody's cellar or garage. She'll be back in another day or so. Our cat was missing for a whole week, once, and finally showed up none the worse for wear."

"But she might have been hit by a car and the body disposed of. Or catnapped. You'd be surprised how many passers-by stop to comment on her size and beauty when she's sunning herself on the front lawn! And another thing, Rom is particularly disturbed about her absence."

A few more words of reassurance, and I wended my way into the den. It seemed good to see Robert back at his work table, and not to hear that interminable click of the machine. Rom greeted me by handing me a sheaf of newly typed pages.

"I thought you might like to read the ending before I mail it off to the magazine."

"But isn't this story going to be too long for Uncanny'?"

"I wrote the editor when I first started it, explaining the project to him, and he answered that if the story was up to what he called my usual high standard he'd change the policy and run it as a three part serial."

I thought the story was superb, and I told him so. The evening flew by all to fast and, except for the absence of Blossom, proved one of the most enjoyable I'd spent at his home so far.

But when I returned the following week, the scene had changed again. Rom was already hard at work on the second book. I watched him carefully, still trying to understand what strange, supernatural power was able to take him over so completely. And why the urgency, the haste. He seemed to be devil-driven, as though he had only a limited time left in which to complete the trilogy, though any sensible reason for such frenetic pressure was beyond my comprehension. As for Blossom, both Aggie and Robert had finally given up all hope of seeing her again, although the why, when and how of her vanishing presented another unsolvable mystery.

And so it went, week after week, all through April, May, and over into June. Rom was beginning to show signs of wear and tear under the strain. His cheeks had deeper hollows beneath the high cheek-bones, dark circles began to show under his eyes, and he was visibly losing weight. And then the project was finished, the third book sent to market, the typewriter pushed back in its place against the wall.

"If I was inclined to be the least bit superstitious," Rom confessed, the week after things seemed to have settled back to a nearer normal routine, "I might be inclined to feel that some of that trilogy was the work of a mind more deeply steeped in demonology and black magic than my own. Particularly in the third book, where the hero in his life and death struggle with the evil forces, postponed his inevitable doom by using incantations and formulas I have no recollection of ever having heard before. I might even let myself think that I could have incurred the enmity of these same bestial beings from beyond, for revealing secrets that might help some mere mortal battle their maleficent machinations on a more equal footing. But, enough of that, or I'll be convincing myself that such things really exit, though common sense tells me it's impossible."

Although I didn't contradict him, I was beginning to have my own doubts. After having been a first-hand observer of the manuscript marathon he'd just completed, I could believe almost anything!

"Now that the weather is mild enough so that I'm in circulation again," Rom continued, "I wonder if I could coax you to give me some extra nights for an experiment I'd like to make. I've been taking trolley trips all over the area, and hearing all sorts of oldwives' tales about haunted houses and ghostly graveyards. There's one place in particular, a town called Granville, about ten miles the other side of Bayboro, that's alive with rumors, but I'll need an automobile to solve the problem of night transportation, and a neutral observer to go along to substantiate my findings. If you'll agree, Biff, I'll get the necessary O.K.'s. How about it?"

Aggie had already confided that Rom had thrown himself into this new project with the same fervor and zeal that had gone into the writing of his trilogy. He was getting very little rest, between doing his regular work at night and touring the countryside by day, but was eating regularly again, and the hours he was spending in the open air and sunshine were putting some color back into his cheeks, which made us both a lot happier.

Frankly I wasn't too enthusiastic over this new idea of his. It was a good fifty miles from Fenham to Bayboro, and most of the road paralleled the famous Witches' Swamp, a treelined monstrosity of nature that varied in width from a mere trickle at either end, to close to a half of a mile at its widest point. Add to this, another ten miles beyond the thriving city of Bayboro, and you came up with a trip I knew I wouldn't relish, particularly when it meant an all night vigil after we finally reached Granville.

However, I could see that Rom was tremendously upset over the ideas that writing the three books had implanted in his mind, and I felt that this new project might have enough therapeutic value to counteract some of the silly thoughts that were upsetting his usual, calm, rational mind. I did not discuss this with him, however; I simply told him to complete his arrangements within the next few days and that when I came over next Tuesday, we would lay out a working schedule.

When I checked in with Rom on the following Tuesday evening I found him as excited as a kid with a brand new toy. It had only taken him two more letters to Granville to complete tentative arrangements. The local realtor had sent him the addresses and keys to three vacant dwellings for which he had been unable to find tenants because of their spook-ridden reputation, and he had checked with the chief of police in town so that he could discount any calls he might receive from jittery neighbors who might think our presence was a new out-break of ghostly visitations. All that remained was a couple of phone calls to alert the real estate broker and the local constabulary as to just what nights we expected so spend there.

The rest of the evening was spent in convincing Rom that it would never do for me to spend five consecutive days and nights away from my own business. I never knew when a call would come in for a job and while both of my assistants were fully capable of doing any work I might assign to them, they were the kind that needed everything spelled out in words of one syllable before they took over, and I must be available to alter my instructions just in case anything unexpected arose. I finally asked Aggie to sit in on the conference, and together we worked out what seemed like a practical plan. Rom and I would go up tomorrow night, and again on Friday. We'd leave the last of the houses until the following Monday, and take the two cemeteries on Wednesday and Friday of the second week. Aggie agreed to phone both Chief Donilon and the real estate office the first thing in the morning and advise them of our schedule.

The very first night we spent in one of the dilapidated dwellings, we were prowling around the upper floor trying to locate one of those eerie sounds that had contributed to frightening off the house's last timorous tenants when, prompted by some sudden impulse, I grasped Rom by the arm and pulled him sharply to one side. I was just in time! The rotten boards on which he had been standing gave way and plunged to the floor below. They would have carried him down with them, had I not acted just in the nick of time!

On our second trip out we spent the night in a more modern structure, but one the realty company could not rent because the last tenant had been murdered and his spirit was still supposed to stalk through the rooms, nightly. We were sitting on either side of the picture window in the front room awaiting developments---if any!

Shortly after midnight the area was hit by one of those severe, fast-moving, July tempests. Lightning struck a huge tree in the yard and toppled it over with enough force to shatter the window. One segment of the glass split into a long, wedgeshaped shard sharp as a bayonet, which stuck upright in the floor at the exact spot where Robert's chair had been located before I pulled it back to save him from being impaled!

The change of pace over the weekend, including a Sunday in which to completely relax, fortified me for a return to Granville on Monday. This was to be our last night in one of the supposed-to-be phantom-filled dwellings. It started off as another of those uneventful sessions of watchful waiting. Both Rom and I were surprised when, just about midnight, Chief Donilon turned up to ask our cooperation.

We had already notified him that out next scheduled stop was the large cemetery located just outside the center of the town. He explained that a new medical college had recently opened in Bayboro, and the students were suspected of collecting cadavers from this particular burial ground. He asked us if we'd keep our eyes open for any trace of such goings on, as well as maintaining our lookout for spectral visitors.

To say that I was pleased at something to break the monotony of another night of watchful waiting would be putting it mildly. The police chief's suggestion that I might actually have a chance to become a hero made me suddenly realize to what extent I had been neglecting my fictional binges since I had been spending so much time with Rom and his inspired writings. At the same time, I knew full well that I would have to forego this pleasure until after this two-weeks episode in Granville had been completed.

The more I thought of it, the more determined I became that these barbaric vandals who sought to violate the sanctity of such a hallowed spot should be apprehended and made to pay to the full extent of the law. My mind was still seething with plans to circumvent them when, shortly before sunset on Wednesday we drove through the gates of Heavenly Rest Cemetery in Granville, and found the caretaker waiting for us in front of his shack just inside the grounds.

That custodian proved to be one garrulous guy! Outside of the time it took him to lock the big double gates at sunset, plus an occasional pause to let some straggler out who had inadvertently been locked in for the night, he kept up a constant stream of chatter 'till close to midnight. He finally excused himself by explaining that he had to open the gates at sunrise, but told us to call him if we needed his help in any way.

Frankly, I didn't hear much of his senseless chatter and let Rom do the heavy listening. I was too busy trying to figure out the best place to station ourselves in order to surprise the grave robbers should they pick tonight to ply their nefarious trade.

Not too far from the main gates, and facing them, was a gigantic statue of an angel with outstretched wings, a veritable colossus, at least nine feet tall. I interrupted the watchman long enough to ask him how such an impressive piece of sculpture happened to be erected there, and why. As I expected, he had all the answers!

Hezekiah Gran, who founded the town, and owned practically everything and everybody in Granville, had donated several acres of his land for use as a graveyard, when the few churchyards had been filled to capacity. On his death, his widow had had the angel constructed to mark his last resting place, until she joined him in the life beyond. Now both bodies were buried in the shadow of its sheltering wings.

This was how I sized up the situation. If the midnight marauders elected to choose tonight for another raid, the best vantage point to await them would be the shaded area around the statue. They could enter the grounds at any point by climbing over the six-foot stone wall which completely surrounded the area but it would be very difficult, once they had exhumed a body to make their exit in the same manner. I reasoned they would unlock the gates with a skeleton key, place the body in a car parked without lights just outside, leaving one of their gang behind to relock the gates, clamber over the stone wall and rejoin his gang. My ratiocination was sound enough, but fate had a more horrific program scheduled for us than the mere apprehension of corpse snatchers!

Again, nothing happened 'till after midnight. I must have been born with some sixth sense of impending disaster. Otherwise I would never have noticed the slight tilting earth which warned me of imminent peril. I barely had time to grab Rom by the arm and literally drag him to the watchman's shack before the full force of the cataclysm hit us.

By the time we succeeded in rousing him, the ground was undulating so violently we could scarcely stand erect. It was Rom, however, with his vast store of knowledge, who recognized it for what it was---an earthquake !

Suddenly, with a reverberation I will never forget, the earth split asunder in an almost straight line from just ahead of the memorial statue, behind which we had been hiding, and extending all the way to the stone wall at the rear.

Tombstones toppled like tenpins and disappeared into

the yawning chasm. The Gargantuan guardian of the graves, after teetering for a long moment of indecision, finally crashed atop the remains of its sponsors into the seemingly bottomless void, which by now was wide enough and deep enough so that the angelic figure dropped completely out of sight!

My one thought was to get out of the place and far away before we, too, were gobbled up by some fresh fissure in the quivering, quavering ground beneath us!

The caretaker was trying, with no success, to unlock the main gates, when I noticed that a section of the stone wall had succumbed to the violent vibrations and was now just a pile of rocky rubble. I gripped both men and partly dragged., partly guided them to and over the debris, onto the solid ground outside. To our mutual surprise, once we left the confines of Heavenly Rest, it was calm and peaceful as though the chaotic confusion inside the gates had never existed!

I offered to drive the caretaker anywhere he wanted to go. He refused, saying that now the quake had subsided, and his shack was still intact, his place was on the grounds where he could start repairing some of the more minor damage left in the wake of the quake! We last saw him laboriously clambering over the debris that was once a part of the encompassing barrier.

If I hadn't been convinced before, I was positive now that we were battling some force beyond human understanding!

It was inconceivable to me that the events of the past few nights were not directed by some malign force intent on destroying Rom for his part in transcribing the secret lore revealed in his trilogy.

I mentally reviewed the events of the nights we had spent to date in Granville. The broken floor boards, the tempest-shattered tree which crashed through the picture window. I believed now that the reason nothing had happened on the third night was because the sheriff had chosen the midnight hour to discuss our future plans. So, tonight, also at the midnight hour, the forces had struck once more, this time more vengefully than ever!

It was a good thing I knew the road so well between Bayboro and Fenham. Once on it, I drove like a veritable demon out of Gehenna, keeping up a running fire of conversation in an effort to point out to Rom that we were faced with a situation that could easily end in our mutual destruction. I begged him to cancel Friday's project, because I had no way of knowing if I could save him should the powers of evil strike again!

I might as well have saved my breath. He pointed out that all these things were explainable by natural means and could, and probably would, have happened had we been miles away.

It is needless to try to depict the many hours of mental misery I spent in trying to conjure up a picture of what might happen to us on our final rendezvous with unknown peril. I only know that by the time we set out for our next appointment with danger, I was inwardly shaken by a vagueness and uncertainty that was new in my experience, and I didn't like it even a little bit !

Robert, on the other hand, was more calm and imperturbable than usual, as if he was prepared to accept any unusual occurrence an another natural phenomenon rather than a manifestation of some super-human control.

Our destination turned out to be an ancient church about a mile beyond the center of Granville, an old-fashioned structure with a steeple which towed high above the modest dwellings in the surrounding area. This steeple housed the giant bell, cast in the days when metal was cheap, whose sonorous tones had summoned the congregation to worship, 'till the faithful parishioners for generations had gone to their last resting places in the churchyard. It was in this hallowed spot, amid the crumbling gravestones, that Rom had decided we should keep our final, all-night vigil.

Robert chose a vantage point just behind the church, facing the markers of the ancient graves, where he would be able to see any signs of materializations that might appear. I, for one, had the distinct feeling that he was in for another evening of disappointment . . . that, instead, we were due for an unmatched night of demoniac inspired terror with its attendant personal peril.

My feelings intensified as we neared the fateful hour of midnight. I let my imagination run riot in an attempt to picture what sort of an attack would be unleashed upon us this time. Meanwhile, I was keeping eyes and ears alert for the first indications of any trouble.

Perhaps a quarter of a mile ahead of us, as we faced the decrepit graves, was a hill which must have risen substantially above any point in the surrounding territory, even higher than the spire of the edifice which hid us from the road. At its very summit stood a pair of giant trees, but because of the height and the distance, they seemed like mere toys. Some unexplainable urgency kept my gaze focused upon them, a steady scrutiny that should have tipped me off as to what lay in store!

Suddenly, soundlessly, the tops of both trees bent backwards almost to the breaking point, as if pressed down by two huge hands. Gradually the branches straightened up again, as the ferocity of the force moved downward and battered the sturdy trunks of the forest giants as if trying to gauge the height at which it wished to operate.

As the level of the wind lowered it seemed to increase in velocity until I could hear the whistle which only accompanies such a storm when it has reached or exceeded hurricane intensity. Yet, unlike any similar disturbance which I had encountered in my many years of voluminous reading, there was no trace of the torrential rains which were usually an integral part of such a gale.

One of the basic differences between Rom and me seemed to be that when he set up a new project for himself, he concentrated to such an extent that he was completely oblivious to all else that was going on around him, and tonight he was intent only on spotting any ghostly goings-on that might be sighted. On the other hand, with my often wild imagination, intensified by a decade and a half of following the fictional fortunes of my favorite heroes on this and other planets, I tried to mentally picture what might happen in this quiet churchyard that could possibly spell peril greater than that which we had faced in the previous nights we had already spent in this damnable town!

All at once I came alive and ready for immediate action! A creaking board in the belfry high overhead made me fully aware that the wind had finally reached a point where it was bringing all its ponderous strength to bear on the tower with its mass of metal which, if it crashed atop us, could be every bit as deadly as the more spectacular demonstration of two nights before!

There was only one thing to do. That was to get out of there as fast as humanly possible. As I gripped Robert firmly by the arm I could hear the timbers splintering above us as the full vehemence of the storm concentrated on destroying the dome.

For once Rom uttered no protest as I guided him safely through the flying boards to the spot, half a block beyond the old churchyard, where I had thoughtfully parked the car. As we clambered aboard we heard the resounding crash, as what was left of the ancient spire and its massive contents landed in the rear of the old church in almost the exact spot where we had been watchfully waiting. We cowered in stunned silence in the sanctuary of the car while the reverberations died away. Not until then did we realize that the stillness was accentuated by the fact that the hurricane-like winds were also gone and the night was as calm as a summer night could be.

As soon as I felt satisfied that Robert had recovered from this last narrow escape from annihilation, I suggested that there was no further need for us to linger any longer in Granville and that I, for one, wanted to head home. As we started on the long road towards Fenham I was surprised to find Rom in a more cheerful frame of mind than he had been since he had suggested this ghost-hunting expedition. It only took an adroit question or two to get him to tell me why. He was completely convinced that he had been right from the beginning---that there was no such thing as an apparition except in the fevered imagination of moronic-minded nitwits.

But I had entirely different ideas on the matter. In my mind no self-respecting spook could hope to compete with the malevolent forces which had been unleashed against us during our two weeks' experiences in Granville. I felt that they would only marshal their resources for a more decisive, more vehement attack in the not-too-distant future. My common sense told me that, for reasons of their own, they wanted it to appear that Rom's demise would have been due to natural causes, and I, alone, had been able to circumvent them single-handed. I coined a phrase which seemed to me to be particularly appropriate to the happenings of the past fortnight. This was only the end of the beginning! It followed in natural sequence to wonder when the next attack would occur---and where---and how!

With Robert quiescent at least for the time being, I allowed myself to try to mentally anticipate the next move or moves of the opposing forces. I only succeeded, however, in conjuring up a string of palpably improbable situations, and when we finally pulled up in front of 31 Spring Lane, I was no nearer a solution than when we started back to Fenham.

The house was pitch dark, except for the single light Agatha had been leaving in the vestibule on these last two weeks of nocturnal expeditions. Rom already had his key in hand, wished me a cheery good night, reminded me that we had a date for the coming Tuesday evening, and strode briskly up the flagstoned path. He let himself in and turned off the night light before he headed for the sanctuary of his workshop, to tackle some of the backlog that must have piled workshop, to tackle some of the backlog that must have piled up during our explorations in Granville.

Then I did something I had never done before. As soon as Rom was safely inside, I shut off both the motor and the headlights and sat alone in the darkened car for close to an hour, just thinking. First of all I wished that Agatha had been awake so that I could discuss the happenings of the last two weeks while they were fresh in my thoughts and find out if she believed, as I did, that the series of occurrences were directed by some superhuman force or if this viewpoint originated only in my fiction-stimulated mind! I don't believe that right up to this moment I had fully appreciated her ability to accurately analyze everything that had transpired, and I longed to have her dispel my doubts with her calm, cool logic and power of reasoning.

Suddenly it struck me with thunderous impact that, as far as Agatha Simmons was concerned, I had never fully appreciated her as a woman, and how much I needed her as a complement to my life. The more I thought about it, the more I realized how difficult it might be, considering her devotion to Rom, to sell her the idea that I should become an essential part of their lives, but I made a decision then and there that I would start working on it at the earliest opportunity!

Finally, my cranium crammed with romantic thoughts, I started the car and drove leisurely home!

The next fortnight was so uneventful it left me with a sort of empty feeling. Of course, there were my regular Tuesday evenings at Rom's, but he was so busy getting squared away with the work that had piled up during the summer that I actually spent more time with Aggie than I did with Robert which, of course, did not hurt my feelings in the least!

Fenham's only newspaper was a semi-weekly, crammed with local jottings covering all the villages from the outskirts of Fenham, in one direction, to Bayboro in the other. Bayboro was our nearest city, and its metropolitan paper boasted both daily and Sunday editions. Although few of our old-timers bought the *Bayboro Daily Blade*, practically everyone in the area purchased the *Bayboro Sunday Blade*, with its comics, its local and national magazine sections, its news of the world and everything that goes to make up an urban publication. Pop Ferguson usually got his advance copies late Saturday afternoon, and I made it a point to pick mine up, rather than wait till some not-too-ambitious paper boy decided to deliver it some time on Sunday!

Everyone has a different way of reading a Sunday paper. I always looked at the "funnies" first. In the last few years, these so-called "comics" had become illustrated serial stories, and to miss an issue was to upset the continuity of the entire series! I followed this with the local magazine section, to see what features the staff reporters had dreamed up that had not already been covered by the myriad of writers who served up current gossip to the readers of our home town paper. Usually a cursory glance was sufficient before I progressed to the national news and features.

This time, however, one of the regional journalists had come up with a yarn which was headlined on the front page of the sections and continues, with photos, on five of the subsequent pages. The writer of the spread, with an imagination rare for a small town scribe, had titled the imagination rare for a small town scribe, had titled the article:

"BLACK NOON"

These two words appeared in letters large enough to occupy the top half of the sheet, and the balance of page one was set all in bold type.

The story went back to just before the turn of the century, when a lumber company, located in the westerly end of the state, had bought the several acres of forest situated on the opposite side of the stagnant, tree-filled gully which paralleled the main highway almost the entire distance from Fenham to Bayboro. There seemed no feasible way to cross this barrier.

The nearest paper mills were located a few miles beyond Bayboro. Reluctant to travel an extra fifty miles or more, first through Fenham, then all the way into the heart of Bayboro, they evolved what seemed to them an ideal solution. They decided to build a road across the morass to eliminate excess travel to their destinations. Why they had picked the only place where Witches' Swamp widened to nearly half a mile, was something none of the older living residents either knew nor could remember.

First the laborers had cut down all the growth from one bank of the swamp to the other, eliminating all extraneous matter from an area wide enough to allow their heavily laden vehicles an easy passageway across.

Next, they used a solid dirt fill, at both ends of the clearing, for about one-and-a-half times the length of the lumber-packed vehicles that were to operate between the terminals. Then they tamped and rolled it down till no sign of seepage showed through, and topped it with a coating of cement for good measure!

The final step was to cut and trim enough logs the exact width of the new highway and lash them together to construct a corduroy road that would span the entire portion of the route between the cement-covered approaches.

As if to protest the invasion of their former privacy, the trees on either side of this new construction had grown so close together that their trunks touched one another, and so tall that their leafy branches had interlocked to form a well-nigh impenetrable covering. In addition, hybrid vines, which grew rampant in the swamp, had over-grown both oaks and branches to eliminate all light from the canopy thus formed. The only thing that could find a way through this natural barrier was the fog which, during the early Fall, hung over the entire swampy area!

Even at high noon, that portion of the road was black as a moon-less midnight! The writer of the article reverted to his title and emphasized his theme of the absence of all illumination from the sheltered section!

The first few days of September were busy ones for me. An unexpected emergency meant that I had to work all day on Sunday, and I completely forgot to wonder if Rom had noticed the feature story in the Sunday Blade and how he might react to it. But when I arrived at 31 Spring Lane, on my regular Tuesday evening visit, I found the whole household in an unusually festive mood. It seemed that both Rom and Aggie had read the article, made their own plans, and taken it for granted that I would be willing to join in wholeheartedly with them! In fact, Robert seemed inclined to censure me for having driven past the entrance to the road across the bog twice each time we made the round trip to Granville, and not having mentioned it to him.

It took me considerable time and effort to convince him that the short-cut through the swampland had been there so many years that I had never given it a second thought, even though I had driven past it hundreds of times in the pursuance of my daily activities. He finally gave in grumpily and he and Aggie went on to outline the activities they had dreamed up for the coming Friday.

All this talk about the excursion on the coming weekend started me off on another chain of disquieting thoughts. Why had this write-up about Witches' Swamp broken at this particular time? Was it another move inspired by the demoniac devils who had been pursuing Rom since he had completed his trilogy? Or was it a strictly unrelated coincidence to which I shouldn't give a second, serious thought? I decided not to even mention it to Robert, although I fully intended to talk it over with Agatha at the first available opportunity.

Once I had convinced Rom that I'd had no ulterior motive in withholding my knowledge of the long unused passageway across the swamp, and while Aggie was busying herself with the more practical phases of the coming expedition, Robert launched into an enthusiastic explanation as to how his trilogy had been received by Bill Laird, the new editor of "Uncanny Stories."

As my grandmother would have expressed it, Rom's tongue seemed to hang in the middle, and wag at both ends!

Robert went on to explain that each time he had mailed a completed segment of the trilogy, Laird had phoned him and heaped praises upon him for the best work he had ever turned out, and told him how much he thought it would mean to the circulation of the magazine once it started to appear. Laird was planning to start it in the April issue and run each hundred-thousand word portion in four, approximately equal-length installments with perhaps a month's leeway between each of the three novels to allow for a build-up in reader interest.

He also agreed to pay Rom at the prevailing top rate of one-half cent a word as each month's portion was published, instead of making him wait until each third of the trilogy had appeared in print. This would assure Robert an average income of well over a hundred bucks a month for the run of three novels, and Rom was already dreaming dreams of how it would feel to have a substantial, dependable income! He talked so incessantly that I was impelled to liken him to Tennyson's brook---the one that ran on forever.

All the while that Robert had been rambling on about his tentative plans concerning his soon to be acquired affluence, a disquieting thought had been gnawing at the back of my mind, but I couldn't seem to bring it to the forefront of my consciousness. Not knowing what was disturbing me bothered me more than the knowledge of it would have. Or so I thought at the time.

It would have kept gnawing at me if Aggie hadn't cut in with some matter-of-fact stuff about the coming expedition.

She asked if I had either galoshes or a pair of knee-high rubber boots to prevent skidding on that part of the passageway that had been hidden all summer by the leafy covering that shut out all sunshine. I told her that my rubber boots were already packed in the car, also that I did not intend to dress up for the trip, but planned to wear an old shirt, cap and overalls as well. Agatha agreed that I was showing good common sense, and told me she had rounded up a pair of seven-buckle overshoes for Rom.

Back at home that evening, my thoughts reverted to the five nights we had spent in Granville. Despite Rom's attempt to attribute all these happenings to natural causes, I couldn't forget how I had literally been his savior on those occasions, those times when he was attacked by the malevolent forces which seemed intent on destroying or crippling Rom, and from which I alone had been able to rescue him.

First was the episode of the rotten floor boards in the first house we visited. The next night was the incident of the lightning-felled tree which crashed through the plate-glass window. Our third night in Granville was free of any untoward incident primarily, I believe, because the chief of police turned up at midnight to discuss our future plans. The fourth night was the one when the cemetery was riven from end to end by an earthquake which carved a cavern from one end of the graveyard to the other, yet no sign of the cataclysm was visible when I finally succeeded in dragging Robert and the terrified caretaker to the safety of the outside world. And, lastly the night in the ancient churchyard where the gale, coming from nowhere, felled the bell-tower with its tons of masonry, and I succeeded in getting Rom out from under in time!

Try as I might, I could not swerve Rom from his deep-rooted belief that all these near misses were due to natural causes, and I was beginning to have serious doubts that anyone or anything would be strong enough to swing him over to my way of thinking! If I could only convert Aggie to my viewpoint, perhaps she could persuade him to change his mind.

But Fate has odd ways of working things out! I don't know what prompted me to show up at Rom's as early as ten on Thursday morning. Aggie was in the front yard, where she had been mowing the lawn. Right now she was staring at a letter she was holding, and she greeted me with such a torrent of words that at first I had difficulty in fully understanding them.

Agatha had dropped the envelope. I picked it up, saw that it was from the editor of "Uncanny Stories" and tucked it safely away in my inside coat pocket. I shook Aggie sharply, and cut in on her incoherent flow of words.

"Slow down, Aggie, and start over again! You're talking so fast that nobody can understand a word you're saying! I know the letter is from Laird, and I assume it's bad news from your reaction to it." I finally calmed her into some semblance of coherency, and she began once more.

"This letter," she explained, "came special delivery only about ten minutes ago. Before I tell you what it's all about, I want your solemn promise you won't even mention it to Rom. I'll tell him the whole story after you folks get back from your trip tomorrow, and he can phone Laird and see if he can make him understand why it would be impossible to duplicate them."

"Duplicate what, Aggie?"

"Laird said the trilogy has been lost. It has disappeared!"

"Disappeared? How could that possibly happen?"

"That seems to be a mystery."

"Or perhaps some supernatural power." My imagination was working again.

I had spent at least one night a week with Rom for the entire fifteen weeks that he was working on the manuscripts, and I know it was as though he was taking dictation from some other world, from some disembodied spirit who was revealing long-buried secrets with which no mortal man should be entrusted! I also know that for the only time in his entire writing career, no copies were made, or kept of the chronicles so that it would be absolutely impossible to recreate them!

Another thought suddenly struck me. Rom's cat, Blossom, had disappeared right after he finished the trilogy. Was that just a coincidence?